# Her heart jumped
# as she met Jackson Miller's eyes.

Even in the midst of her terror, half-frozen and desperate, she recognized him. She'd dreamed about him dozens of times.

"Are you okay?" he asked. "You're looking a little pale."

"I'm fine." She met his eyes, her pulse jumping again. He was as handsome as she'd remembered. "But you..." She touched a bruise that was forming on his cheekbone.

"Must have happened when I jumped out of the way of the Jeep that was trying to run me down." He watched her steadily as he spoke. "You know anyone with a blue Jeep?"

"No."

"You're sure, because someone was in the woods with you."

Fear clogged her throat. She'd been trying to convince herself that she'd imagined the man and his whispered threat. That everything that had happened since she'd woken to a child's cries had been part of some bizarre dream.

It wasn't, though. It was real. And someone wanted to hurt her.

# PROTECTIVE INSTINCTS

## SHIRLEE MCCOY

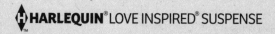

LOVE INSPIRED BOOKS

ISBN-13: 978-0-373-67617-0

PROTECTIVE INSTINCTS

www.Harlequin.com

For I know the plans I have for you, declares the Lord, plans to prosper you and not to harm you, plans to give you hope and a future.

—*Jeremiah* 29:11

To Glenda Winters, because she knows how to hold on and how to let go. Blessings to you, my friend. And prayers that God will give you comfort and courage and peace.

# PROLOGUE

*Sudan*
*Six months ago*

Dying felt like summer heat and dusty earth. It sounded like flies and buzzards, humming and flapping in Raina Lowery's ears as she lay on the hot, hard ground of the African savanna.

*Please, God, just let it end soon.* The prayer flitted through her mind. There and gone so quickly she couldn't quite grab hold of it.

Close by, someone groaned, the sound drifting on waves of scorching heat. Twenty days traveling rugged terrain with little water, five days lying in cages in the blazing sun. They'd all die soon. Some of them already had.

Of the ten-member missionary team, seven had survived the initial attack against the small village where they'd been staying. Only five of the remaining had completed the forced journey to the rebel encampment.

Raina didn't know how many more had died since they'd arrived. If any of them lived, it would be a miracle, and she'd given up believing in those years ago.

A fraud trying to live a faith that she'd professed when she was a child; that's what she'd felt like when she'd agreed to travel with the medical mission. She'd die a fraud, because she hadn't found what she'd been looking for when she'd left Pine Bluff, Washington, and flown to Africa.

*Dear God, please...*

Something rustled beside her, and she opened her eyes, squinting against the late-afternoon sun. A gun strapped to his shoulder, his eyes hollow and old, a boy soldier peered through the cage bars. Young. Six or seven. A year or two younger than Joseph would have been. His close-cropped hair was coated with dirt, his cheeks covered with grime. He wore a baggy shirt and faded red shorts. His feet were bare.

Raina thought that he'd spit on her the way others had, but he pulled an old water bottle from beneath his baggy black T-shirt and slid it through the bars.

"Drink," he whispered, his English thick and heavily accented.

She wanted to thank him, but her tongue stuck to the roof of her mouth, and she couldn't get the words out. She lifted the murky water and drank greedily, gulping it down so quickly she almost choked.

She passed the bottle back through the bars, desperate for more. But the boy shoved it back under his shirt and ran off.

Alone again, she curled into a fetal position, the hot earth burning her cheek, the water roiling in her stomach. The buzzards flapped their wings, the droning sounds of the flies growing so loud they were almost deafening.

The air hung still and heavy, the heat so thick she could taste it on the back of her tongue, feel it in the sluggish pulse of her blood. It dragged at her, pulling her down into a darkness she wasn't sure she'd ever escape.

Someone shouted and gunfire blasted through the encampment, the explosive power of machine-gun rounds vibrating through the hard ground. Raina pushed to her knees, couldn't make it to her feet. Fire blazed from the roof of one of the rebel's huts, the shimmering heat dancing against the afternoon sky. A black helicopter hovered above, blowing the smoke and flames into a frenzy of motion. Men ran toward the tall savanna grasses, weapons slapping against narrow backs, boots thudding on drought-dry earth.

A small figure darted through the chaos,

running straight toward Raina's prison. Black T-shirt and old red shorts, skinny legs pumping hard. No gun this time. Just wild fear in his ancient eyes.

He crouched near the cage door, his hand shaking as he shoved a key into the padlock.

"You have to run and hide!" Raina tried to shout, but her voice caught in her parched throat, and all that came out was a croak.

The door swung open, and the boy held out his hand. "You are free."

Their gazes locked, and she reached for him, her fingers brushing the warm, dry tips of his.

Another explosion, and his eyes went wide as he fell into the cage.

"No!" Raina rasped, not caring about the open door that he'd fallen through, the war raging behind him. A rebel soldier lay a dozen yards away, blood pooling beneath him, the gun he'd used to bring down the boy lying near his outstretched hand. All Raina cared about was the boy. She touched his neck, felt his thready rapid pulse.

Her training kicked in then. All the years of being an emergency room nurse drove her to action. Blood spurted from the boy's leg. The injury to his thigh was so severe, she didn't think the limb could be saved. She ripped off a piece of her shirt, tied it around the top of his leg to cut off blood flow. It was that or watch him die.

He couldn't have weighed more than fifty pounds, but Raina struggled to lift him and stagger out of the cage. Dizzy, disoriented, she aimed for the tall grass, stumbling past the rebel's body. Heat blazed from the raging fire and the endless sun. Her arms and legs trembled, but she couldn't stop, couldn't put the boy down.

*Please, God...*

*Please...*

Her legs gave out, and she tumbled backward, her arms still wrapped around the boy. He groaned, his dark eyes staring into hers, blank but still lit with life and hope.

*Please.*

"It's okay. You're safe now. We're going to get you home," a man said, crouching beside her, his tan pants and long-sleeved shirt crisp and clean, his accent the deep drawl of a true Southerner. Deep blue eyes and an unyielding face. Hard edges and sharp angles and a scar that split one dark eyebrow.

*Who are you?* she thought, the words trapped in her head, unable to escape the fiery heat in her throat, the dryness of her mouth.

"Let's get out of here." He tried to pull her from the boy, but she tightened her grip.

"No."

"We can't bring him with us. There's no room on the chopper." His voice was as gentle as sunrise, and Raina wanted to close her eyes, release her grip, let herself fall into the care he seemed to be offering.

She couldn't leave the boy, though.

*Wouldn't.*

"Take *him,* then." She thrust the boy into his arms, her muscles trembling, blackness edging at the corner of her mind. Maybe this was where she was meant to die. Maybe four years of searching for the faith she'd lost had led her straight into God's arms.

She swayed, so ready to give in that her knees buckled.

"Don't give up now," he growled, his free arm snaking around her waist. He pulled her upright, and she had no choice but to run beside him. It was that or drag all three of them down.

"Jackson! Hurry it up. We've got heat coming in from the west." A woman raced toward them, her blond hair pulled into a ponytail, a gun strapped to her chest. She wore the same uniform as the man. A blue heart was stitched on one shoulder.

"Everyone is accounted for?"

"If this is Raina, then yes." The woman offered Raina a kind smile that didn't quite fit the hard angles and edges of her face. Her gaze dropped to the boy, and she frowned. "We can't take him. You know that, right?"

"Rules are meant to be broken, Stella. Isn't that your philosophy of life?"

"True." She took the boy from his arms. "Let's get out of here."

She ran toward a waiting helicopter, dust and debris swirling, her blond ponytail flying. Raina wanted to run, too, but she couldn't feel her feet, her legs, her body. Didn't know if she was standing or lying down. Hazy sky and yellow sun and midnight-blue eyes. The endless flap of buzzard wings.

"You're going to be okay, Raina," someone whispered as she slid into darkness.

# ONE

*Help me, Mommy. Please! Help me!*

The cries drifted into Raina's consciousness, weaving their way through vivid dreams: Africa. A young boy who wasn't Joseph, but who could have been. Hot sun. Desperate thirst. Fear.

And that cry!

*Help me, Mommy! Please! Help me!*

She jerked awake, her heart thundering so loudly, she thought she was still hearing the cries.

She *was* still hearing the cries.

Wasn't she?

She scrambled out of bed, the sheets and blanket dropping onto the floor, her flannel pajamas tangled around her waist and legs. Wind rattled the windows, the darkness beyond the single-pane glass complete. She cocked her head to the side, heard the house creaking, ice pattering on the roof. Other than that, there was nothing. Her hand shook as she brushed bangs from her

forehead and tried to take a few deep breaths.
Tried, but her lungs wouldn't fill.

"Calm down!" she muttered. "It was just a
dream, and you're still waking up from it."

It wasn't as if she hadn't had the dream many
times in the six months since she'd returned
from the mission trip, and it wasn't as if she
hadn't learned how to deal with it.

She paced to the window then back to the
bed, inhaling, exhaling, forcing herself to relax.

She'd spent the past thirty hours wondering
how the young boy who'd given her a drink of
water and unlocked her cage was faring. Was it
any wonder that she'd had such a vivid nightmare? After fighting red tape and bureaucracy,
petitioning, begging, pleading and pulling every
string she could think of, Raina had finally managed to get him to the United States on a medical visa. He'd stepped onto U.S. soil the previous
morning. The flight from L.A. to Atlanta had
gone off without a hitch, but the flight from Atlanta to D.C. had been canceled.

Good thing Raina had hired an escort to bring
Samuel to the United States. One she trusted im-
plicitly. Stella Silverstone worked for HEART,
the hostage rescue team that had risked everything to save her and the rest of the mission
team. Stella had been brusque and to the point
when she'd called to tell Raina about the delay.

They were stuck in Atlanta, their flight canceled because of the storms. Samuel was fine. Stella would call again when they got a flight out.

That had been more than twelve hours ago.

Raina hadn't heard a word since. She was worried about Samuel. His leg had been amputated above the knee, and he'd suffered reoccurring infections in the stump. He'd been hospitalized for a few weeks before his trip to the United States, and the doctors hadn't been hopeful for his recovery. No wonder Raina was having nightmares.

"But now you're awake, so do something productive instead of standing around panicking." Her words echoed in the room she'd once shared with Matt. Like everything else since the accident that had taken her husband and son, the room seemed to be nothing more than a shadow of its former self. Wedding pictures hung crooked on the wall. Family photos lined the dresser, their frames covered with dust. The pretty yellow bedspread that had been a wedding gift was faded to a muted ivory.

Destiny had tried to get her to redecorate, but Raina hadn't seen the point, so she'd ignored her best friend's suggestions. Now that Matt was gone, the room was just a place to sleep. Half the time, she lay on the couch, watching TV until she finally drifted off.

Matt wasn't around to gently shake her shoulder and laugh while she grumbled about not wanting to get up. He wasn't there to usher her into their room and nuzzle her neck while she pulled down the covers.

It had been years, and she should be used to that, but she wasn't.

She left the room that suddenly seemed too full of memories, and walked down the short hall into the great room. That had been Matt's name for it. It was really nothing more than an oversize living room that had been created when the former owner had combined a formal living and dining area. Matt had lots of big ideas, lots of beautiful ways of looking at the ordinary. She missed his optimistic perspective, but she'd been trying to move on, to create something for herself that didn't include all the dreams that had died when Matt and Joseph had been taken away from her.

She pulled back the curtains and stared out into the tiny front yard. The property butted up against a dirt road that dead-ended a half mile to the west. A century ago, the area had been dotted with farms and orchards, the nearby town of Middletown, Maryland, a bustling community of businessmen and farmers. The Great Depression had hit it hard, but it had rebounded in the 1980s when yuppies willing to take on a long commute had moved there from the Baltimore and Washington suburbs. Farther west, though, where farms had once been the livelihood of the town, abandoned properties and fallow acreage had proven a deterrent to the area's revitalization. Matt had seen it as a blessing, but that was the way he'd always been. Focused on the positive. Willing to work hard to make dreams a reality. He'd seen the old farmhouse and twenty acres of overgrown orchards as an answer to prayer.

Raina had gone along for the ride. Just as she always had, because she'd loved Matt, and she'd wanted what he'd wanted. Now, of course, she was stuck on twenty acres in the middle of nowhere. No close neighbors to visit on the weekends or children playing basketball or hockey on the street. Just Larry, and he stuck close to his house and his property.

Something moved in the early-morning darkness, and she leaned closer to the glass. Probably just a deer. This far out, she saw plenty of them. There were coyotes, too. An occasional bear that wandered in from the deep woodland and hill country. The thing crossed the yard, heading toward Larry's property. No streetlights illuminated the shape, but she was sure it was a biped. Too small to be a bear. A man?

She flicked on the outside light. The shadow darted across the street, disappearing into heavy shrub.

Larry?

She hoped not. Two days ago, he'd been outside barefoot, walking up the road. She'd spotted him on her way home from work at the medical clinic. He'd said he'd been heading to his mailbox at the head of their road, but that hadn't explained the bare feet in fifty-degree weather.

She grabbed the phone and dialed his number, knowing that he wouldn't answer. He never did. That was the thing about Larry. He wanted to be left alone, but if he was outside, he could freeze to death before anyone ever realized he was in trouble.

She yanked on jeans, pulled a coat over her flannel nightie and shoved her feet into boots.

The flashlight was still where Matt had always left it—tucked on the top shelf of the closet with a first-aid kit, a box of candles and matches and a stack of blankets. If Matt had been an outdoorsman, she might have a shotgun to take, too, but he'd been more of an academic, country living more a dream than a reality he'd been prepared to deal with.

She'd been the practical one in their relationship, the one who thought of things like bears and bobcats, who'd built the chicken coop that now stood empty. She'd taught Matt how to camp, fish and even hunt. Not that they'd ever been successful at any of those things. Matt's idea of camping was staying in a hotel near hiking trails, and his vision of hunting had never included actually shooting anything.

She smiled at the memories, touching the bear spray she kept in her coat pocket. Better safe than sorry. It was cold for early November, the temperature well below freezing, ice coating the grass and trees. It took five long strides to cross the front yard, the wind snatching her breath and chilling her cheeks. Across the street, Larry McDermott's house stood shadowy and dark. Shrouded by overgrown trees and a hedge that had probably been planted in the 1950s, it was a Gothic monstrosity that looked as worn and mean as its seventy-year-old owner.

*Not mean,* she could almost hear Matt whisper. *Lonely.*

Maybe. In the years since Matt's and Joseph's deaths, Raina had tried to be kind to her neighbor. For Matt's sake, she'd baked him bread, invited him for Thanksgiving and Christmas. She'd shoveled his driveway after snowstorms and checked in on him when she hadn't seen him for a few days. No matter what she did, he never seemed to warm up to her.

She walked to the edge of his property and made her way along his driveway. Her flashlight beam bounced over cracks in the pavement and illuminated the three stairs that led to Larry's front door. She jiggled the doorknob, knocked twice, wondering if Larry would hear if he were asleep. Her fingers were freezing, but she wanted to check the back door, too. She swept the flashlight across the front yard, her pulse jumping as it passed over what looked like footprints in the icy grass. Instead of thick ice, a thin layer of slush coated the grass there. She scanned the area, found another set of prints near the edge of the house.

"Larry!" she screamed, her voice carried away by the wind. "Larry! Are you out here?" She rounded the side of the house, following the footprints to a gate that banged against the fence with every gust of wind.

"Larry!" She tried one last time, her flashlight tracking footprints to the edge of the woods that separated Larry's yard from the church his grandfather had pastored. The church Matt had pastored for five years before his death. Their home away from home. The only church Joseph had ever known. She knew the path that cut through the woods so well she wouldn't have needed her flashlight to follow it. She used it anyway, making sure that the footprints didn't veer off into the woods.

Larry couldn't be too far ahead.

*If* it was Larry.

She glanced back, could see nothing but white-crusted trees.

She walked another half mile. She'd reach the church parking lot soon, and then what would she do? The place was closed for the night. She was already near frozen. She'd be all the way frozen by the time she walked to the church.

This was a stupid idea. A colossally stupid one. She needed to go back to the house and call the police. If Larry was out in the cold, they'd find him. The problem was, she couldn't stand the thought of her crotchety old neighbor freezing to death while she cowered in her house. She couldn't stomach the idea of one more person dying because she hadn't been able to offer the help he needed.

"Larry!" she shrieked, her words seeming to echo through the woods. The trees grew sparser as she neared the church, and she flashed her lights toward the end of the trail, hoping to catch sight of the older man. Suddenly, a figure stepped out from behind a tree. Not stooped and old like Larry. Tall and lean. Her light flashed on thick ski pants. It glanced off a heavy black parka, landed straight on a black ski mask and glittering eyes that could have been any color.

"Who are you?" she said, her voice wobbling. "What are you doing out here?"

"Go home!" he hissed, pulling something from his pocket.

No. Not something. A handgun. He lifted it, pointed it straight at her head.

"Go!" he repeated, shifting the barrel a fraction of an inch and pulling the trigger.

The night exploded, a bullet whizzing past her head and slamming into a tree. She dodged to the left, dashing into trees as another bullet slammed into the ground behind her.

She tumbled down a small hill, pushed through a thicket. Behind her, branches cracked and feet slapped against frozen earth. He was following her!

She didn't know where she was, where she was heading. She knew only that she had to run. If she didn't, the death she'd avoided in Africa was going to find her.

"This wasn't one of your better ideas, Stel," Jackson Miller muttered as he maneuvered the SUV along an icy dirt road that led to Raina Lowery's house.

"Shh!" Stella responded. "You're going to wake the kid."

"Avoiding the comment doesn't negate it," he replied without lowering his voice. "Besides, Samuel slept through your rendition of 'Take Me Home, Country Roads.' I think he can probably sleep through anything."

"You could be right. My mom once told me that my voice could wake the dead."

"Did she also tell you that driving down icy country roads in the middle of the night could *turn* you into one of the dead?"

Stella laughed. "My mother was all about the thrill. She would have loved this, and you would have loved her. She was crazier than I am."

He doubted it. Stella had a reputation at HEART—hard-core, tough, determined and absolutely fearless. A former army nurse, she handled stress well, and in the four years he'd known her, she'd never caved under pressure. "Most of the time, I like your kind of crazy, Stella, but the next time you want to go for a country ride in the middle of an ice storm, call my brother."

The silence that ensued told Jackson everything he needed to know. Stella and Chance hadn't worked things out.

He hadn't expected them to. They were both as stubborn as mules. The fact that they'd dated at all still surprised him. The fact that his brother, a consummate bachelor, had bought an engagement ring had shocked him. Stella and Chance's breakup four weeks ago? Not surprising at all.

"I didn't call you," Stella finally said. "I stopped by your place. I wouldn't have done that if Samuel hadn't had to use the bathroom."

"Sure. Go ahead and blame it on the kid who's asleep in the backseat," he responded, and Stella laughed again.

"Okay. So I didn't want to come all the way out to Podunk Town alone. Country roads are creepy."

"You've been to some of the most dangerous cities in the world, and you think *this* is creepy?"

"Every ghost story I've ever heard has taken place on a country r—"

Someone darted out of the woods, and Jackson slammed on the brakes. The tires lost traction, and the SUV spun. Jackson managed to turn into the spin, get the vehicle back under control. It coasted to a stop an inch from a giant oak tree.

"What was that?" Stella yelled into the sudden stillness.

"A person." He unbuckled his seat belt, praying for all he was worth that he hadn't hit whoever it was.

"Where'd he go?"

"I don't—"

A woman appeared beside the car. Hair

cropped short and plastered to her head, black coat hanging open to reveal what looked like a flannel pajama top. Jeans. Plastic rain boots. A face that was so familiar his breath caught.

*Raina.*

It had been over six months since he'd seen her, but her image had been carved into his memories so deeply that it seemed like yesterday. He'd been on dozens of rescues, brought plenty of people to safety. He hadn't forgotten any of them, but Raina had been different. He hadn't just remembered her; he hadn't been able to get her out of his mind.

"Help me!" she begged, glancing over her shoulder, her eyes wild with fear. "There's someone chasing me."

He opened the door, scanning the woods behind her. "Who?"

"I don't know. He had a gun. He tried to shoot me." Her teeth were chattering, and he dropped his coat around her shoulders and bundled her into the car.

She grabbed his wrist before he could turn away, her hands cold against his skin. "We need to call the police."

"Okay," he responded, meeting Stella's eyes. Raina didn't seem to know who either of them was. Her lips were pale from cold, rivulets of water streaming down her cheeks and neck.

She'd been outside for a while, and she seemed to be suffering the effects of it. "Tell me what's going on."

"I told you. Someone was chasing me through the woods." She glanced at the trees, her eyes widening. "There, look!"

He whirled in the direction she'd indicated, his hand resting on the gun strapped to his chest. All he saw were trees and deep shadows. "I don't…"

His voice trailed off. Something *did* seem to be moving through the forest. Stella must have seen it, too. She leaned toward him. "You want to check it out, or you want me to?"

"I'll go." He grabbed a flashlight from the glove compartment and headed toward the trees, moving quickly and quietly, the patter of icy rain enveloping him as he entered the woods. It had been years since he'd been hunting, but he knew what to look for. Tracks in the ice, broken branches. He could clearly see the path Raina had taken, the slippery progress she'd made. She'd run haphazardly, zigzagging through foliage.

He moved deeper into the trees, the stillness of the woods broken only by the murmur of leaves and the soft whistling of the wind. The storm seemed to be dying down, the ice turning to a gentle rain. He pushed through a thicket and found himself on a dirt path that ran east and west. West led to the road and the SUV, so he headed east, his light illuminating the slushy path. He could make out footprints, all of them indistinct. Other than that, the dirt yielded nothing.

The path opened into a parking lot, a small church at the far end of it glowing grayish-white in the gloom. A Jeep sat near the tree line a hundred yards away. Dark-colored, the windows tinted, it had a thin layer of ice covering the roof and so much dirt on the license plate it couldn't be read.

He moved toward it, the hair on the back of his neck standing on end. He knew the feeling of impending danger. What six years as a U.S. marine hadn't taught him about it, five years working for HEART had.

Someone was in the car.

He was as sure of it as he was of his own name.

He kept his firearm loose in his right hand, tucked the flashlight into his coat pocket and pulled out his cell. He snapped two pictures of the Jeep and was getting ready to take a third when the engine coughed. Black exhaust poured from the muffler, but instead of speeding out of the parking lot, the driver backed up and pointed the Jeep straight at Jackson.

He dove for cover, tree branches snagging

his coat and ripping into his face as the Jeep slammed into the trees behind him. Leaves and water rained down on his head, blurring his vision as he dropped the cell phone, pivoted and fired his Glock.

# TWO

*If the perp escapes, Chance isn't going to let me live this down.* I'm *not going to let myself live it down.*

Those were Jackson's first thoughts as he fired a second shot at the tires of the fleeing vehicle. The tire blew, the Jeep swerving and righting itself as the driver stepped on the gas and raced away.

He wouldn't get far.

Not in the Jeep.

He might get somewhere on foot. Jackson didn't know the area well, and he wasn't sure how far they were from a main thoroughfare. He ran out into the street, watching as the Jeep's taillights dipped and swerved along the country road. No streetlights to speak of, but Jackson could see a small town in the distance.

If the Jeep was heading in that direction, it should be easy enough to track down. Jackson jogged back to the tree line, flashing his light on the giant oak the Jeep had hit. Bits of bark had sheared off and specks of dark blue paint stuck to the wood. Evidence for the police to collect. Jackson left it alone, careful not to step on tread marks deeply engraved in the muck at the edge of the blacktop. The last thing he needed was to get in deep with the local P.D. The fact that he'd fired his Glock was going to cause problems enough.

Problems that Jackson wanted to handle without any help from Chance.

Not that he didn't appreciate his older brother's input and advice, but Chance got a little too involved sometimes. He worried a little too much. Since they'd lost Charity, everyone in the family did.

His cell phone rang, the sound muffled. He followed it to a pile of ice and leaves, dug through the dirty mess and pulled out the phone.

"Hello?"

"Where are you, Jackson?" Chance's shout cut through the quiet.

"In a church parking lot just outside of a little town called—"

"River Valley," Chance cut him off. "Where's the church? Stella said—"

"You two are finally on speaking terms again?" He tried to change the subject, because he wasn't in the mood for one of his brother's lectures, and because a police car was pulling into the parking lot. Sirens off, lights on, it moved toward him slowly.

"We're always on speaking terms when it comes to work. Delivering Samuel Niag to Raina is work. Chasing people through the woods in unfamiliar territory is not."

"Maybe not," Jackson responded lightly. No sense in getting into it with Chance. Not when he was pretty certain he was about to get into it with River Valley law enforcement.

The officer got out of the car, face shrouded by the rim of his uniform hat. "Keep your hands where I can see them," he growled.

Jackson obliged, lifting both hands in the air, his brother's voice still audible.

"You have any weapons on you?" The officer asked, his gaze on Jackson's shoulder holster and the gun that was visible in it.

"Just my Glock," he responded.

"You have a permit?"

"In my SUV."

"Which is where?" The officer stayed neutral, but he was moving in closer, and Jackson could sense the tension in his shoulders and back, the nervous energy that wafted through the darkness.

Jackson rattled off Raina's address, and the

officer nodded. "I'm going to have to take your firearm until your permit can be verified."

Apparently the officer also had to handcuff Jackson and stick him in the back of the police cruiser while he looked around, because that's exactly where Jackson found himself. Sitting on a cold leather seat, the smell of urine and vomit filling his nose. He'd been in worse situations, been in a lot more danger, but he still didn't like it. Not when the guy who'd tried to run him down was making his escape.

He would have been happy to tell the police officer that, but the guy was a few feet away from the cruiser, speaking into his radio as he scanned the parking lot.

An SUV pulled in. Not just any SUV. The brand-new one Jackson had purchased to replace his old Chevy truck. Chance must have called Stella. She got out of the vehicle and stalked to the police officer's side, her close-cropped hair barely moving in the wind. Used to be, she'd had shoulder-length hair. That was before she and Chance had called it quits. Seconds later, Raina exited the SUV and opened the back door. Samuel slid out, an old wooden crutch under one arm, a giant coat wrapped around his shoulders.

He was tiny for ten, his cheeks gaunt from illness, his jeans hanging loosely, one pant leg rolled up and pinned beneath his stump. See-

ing him after so many months had only made
Jackson regret leaving him in Kenya more than
he had the day he'd flown home. He'd left hundreds of dollars for the young boy's care, and
he'd planned on keeping tabs on Samuel, making sure that he got what he needed to survive
and thrive.

Raina had stepped in first, making phone calls
from her hospital room, transferring money,
doing everything a mother might do for a child
stuck in a foreign land. Jackson had heard all
about it, had followed the news stories about
Raina's fight to get a medical visa for Samuel,
about the offers from medical experts in D.C.
who'd promised surgery and state-of-the-art
prostheses for the child if he could be brought
to the United States.

Raina put a hand under Samuel's elbow, but
the boy shrugged away, determined, it seemed,
to make his way across the still-slick parking
lot himself. The police officer moved toward
them, said a few words that Jackson was really
desperate to hear.

Raina nodded, then gestured to the church.

Seconds later, she and Samuel were moving toward the building. She opened the church
door, allowed Samuel to walk in front of her. The
door closed, and they were gone, lights spilling

out from tall windows and splashing across the parking lot.

Jackson wanted to follow. It was impossible to know if the church was empty. If it was always left unlocked, anyone could be inside, sleeping in the sanctuary on a pew, hiding in a restroom until dawn. Lying in wait for a victim.

The cruiser door opened, and Stella peered in, her eyes gleaming with amusement. "I see you've found your way into trouble again."

"I didn't find it. It found me." He glanced at the officer standing behind her. The guy seemed more focused on the notebook he was writing in than on the crime scene.

"That's always your story, Jack." Stella sighed, grabbing his arm and tugging him from the car. "Hear you lost your Glock."

"I had it confiscated, and I wouldn't mind having it back."

"I wouldn't mind knowing exactly why you decided to fire it," the officer responded without looking up. "I found two bullet casings. You forgot to mention that you'd fired shots."

"You didn't give me a chance."

"You've got one now." He finally met Jackson's eyes. "Want to explain what happened?"

"Someone tried to run me down. I tried to stop him."

"By putting a bullet in him?"

"By putting a bullet in his tire. Which I managed to do. You should find a late model Jeep with a blown tire somewhere nearby. There's a photo of it on my cell phone."

The officer nodded, but didn't look as though he was any closer to letting Jackson out of handcuffs.

"I don't suppose that it occurred to you to do what the pastor of this church did when he heard gunfire—call for help?"

"It occurred to me, but I was occupied with trying to keep myself from being crushed by a Jeep."

That got a smile out of the guy. "Fair enough. I'll call in an APB on the Jeep, see if we can find it and our guy. Want to show me that photo?"

"Want to get me out of these cuffs?"

"Sure, but don't get the idea you're going anywhere. I have some more questions for you." Jackson nodded his agreement and stood still while the handcuffs were being removed. What he really wanted to do was go into the church and make sure Raina and Samuel were okay.

As he handed the officer his cell phone, he glanced at the building. Its pretty white siding and colorful stained glass gleamed in the darkness. A beautiful little building that had probably been standing for generations, but that didn't mean it was safe. One thing Jackson had learned

in his time in the military and with HEART—
the places that should be safest were often the
most dangerous of all.

It had been nearly four years since Raina had
last stepped foot in River Valley Community
Church. She hadn't stopped attending because
her faith had been shaken after Matt and Joseph died. She hadn't stopped because her best
friend had invited her to a new church in town.
One that had lots of young people and plenty of
upbeat music and was designed to make people
feel good about their lives and their faith.

She'd stopped attending because it had been
too hard to keep going.

Too hard to sit in a pew and listen while Pastor William Myer preached. Too hard to listen to
his wife play the piano Raina had once played.
Too hard to be there and not remember the years
she and Matt had served together.

Too hard, and she'd been too weak, too sad,
too *destroyed* by what had happened. Too over-
whelmed by her guilt and her inability to forgive
God and herself.

She touched the vestibule wall, remembering the way she and Matt had laughed as they'd
painted sunny yellow over the mud-brown that
had been there since the 1960s. They'd wanted
to see the old church shine again, and they had.

Matt would say that was a blessing. To Raina it was just another memory that she'd rather forget.

Water ran in the sink, the door to the church's only bathroom still firmly closed. She wanted to knock and make sure that Samuel was okay, but she didn't think he'd appreciate it. He hadn't seemed to want her help, hadn't wanted to talk. He'd been traveling for thirty-six hours, and he was tired and ill. Stella had said he'd been running a 103-degree fever, and that the wound on his stump was seeping and infected. All those things needed to be dealt with, but first Raina had to get him home.

That's where she'd wanted to go.

Straight back to the house. But Stella had had to make a call, then she'd asked if there was anything on the other side of the woods. The next thing Raina had known, they'd been heading for the old church.

She touched the wall again, a million memories flooding her mind and her eyes. It had been a while since she'd cried over what she'd lost, and she didn't plan to cry now, but she couldn't stop thinking about the dream that had woken her. The hot African sun and the little boy crying for help.

The vestibule door opened, cold fall air drifting in and carrying the scent of wood fires and wet leaves. Her favorite time of year, but it seemed as if she'd missed every moment of every fall for the past four years. As if she'd just drifted through the seasons without even noticing the leaves changing color, the snow dusting the ground, the first tulips of spring.

She turned, letting the cold moist air kiss her cheeks and ruffle her hair. She expected Stella to walk through the open door, but the figure that moved into the vestibule was tall and masculine. Her heart jumped as she met Jackson Miller's eyes. Even in the midst of her terror, even half-frozen and desperate, she'd known who he was. She'd recognized the sharp angles of his face, the scar that sliced through his eyebrow, the broadness of his shoulders. She'd dreamed about him dozens of times, relived her captivity and her rescue every day for months.

Yes. She'd have known Jackson anywhere, anytime, in any situation.

"Everything okay in here?" he asked, his Southern drawl as warm as sunlight on a summer morning. It had been months since she'd heard it, but she hadn't forgotten the thick twang, or the way it reminded her of home and safety and freedom.

"Yes." She looked away from his searching gaze. "I'm just waiting for Samuel."

"You've been waiting a long time."

"He's sick and exhausted. Everything takes longer under those circumstances."

"I guess so." He knocked on the door. "Hey, Sammy! You about done in there?"

"He doesn't—" She was going to say *speak much English,* but Samuel poked his head out of the bathroom, his face and hair wet.

"I am finished."

"What'd you do, kid? Take a bath?" Jackson stepped into the bathroom and came back out with a handful of paper towels. He dabbed at Samuel's head and his face, swiped water off the back of his neck, pausing for just a moment at a ridge of scars just below Samuel's hairline. When the young boy tensed, Jackson moved on, finishing the job with quick, efficient movements that Raina envied.

*She* could have been the one helping. She probably should have been the one. After all, she'd be Samuel's caregiver for the next year. She felt awkward, though. As if losing Joseph had caused her to lose every bit of maternal instinct she had.

"Good enough!" Jackson proclaimed with a smile that eased the hardness from his face. "We have to stay here a few more minutes while the police officer collects some evidence. You want to sit down?"

He didn't wait for Samuel to reply, just

scooped him up with his crutch and placed him on a pew at the front of the sanctuary. The young boy looked surprised, but didn't protest. Maybe he was more used to men than women. Or maybe he just sensed the difference between Jackson and Raina—one was relaxed and open, the other tense and closed in and scared.

She had to get over it.

No one had twisted her arm or begged her to help Samuel. She'd come up with the idea all on her own, because she owed him her life. She hadn't been able to forget that, hadn't wanted to. The problem was, she didn't know how to care for a young boy. Not anymore. She knew it, and Samuel seemed to know it.

That was a shame, because she'd really wanted to hit it off with him, to make him feel comfortable and at home.

What she hadn't wanted was to think about Joseph every time she looked into Samuel's face, but she couldn't seem to help herself. They looked nothing alike, but when she looked into Samuel's eyes, she was reminded of Joseph. When she touched his arm, she thought of her son.

"You should probably sit down, too," Jackson said quietly. "You're looking a little pale."

"I'm fine." She met his eyes, felt something in her heart spring to attention. He was as handsome as she'd remembered. As tall. As muscular. He was exactly what she'd have imagined if someone had told her there was a team of people who'd devoted their lives to rescuing the kidnapped, the lost, the wounded from dangerous situations.

"Fine doesn't mean you're not going to fall over faster than Grandma Ruth during a summer revival meeting."

"Your grandmother faints during revival meetings?" she asked, plopping down next to Samuel because her legs were feeling a little weak. She wanted to blame it on fear and stress, but it had more to do with that little ping in her heart when she'd met Jackson's gaze.

"Only when it's hot and she hasn't had enough water."

"You're making that up," she accused, and he smiled, dropping onto the pew beside her.

"Not even a little. The fact is Grandma Ruth has fainted once or twice during revival meetings, and we have to take care to keep her hydrated. The other fact is you look pale as paper, and you really did need to sit down."

"At least I'm not beaten up and bruised," she responded, touching a bump that had formed on his cheekbone. His skin felt warm and just a little rough, and she had the absurd urge to linger there.

She let her hand drop away, and he touched the bruise. "Guess I ran into something while I was avoiding the Jeep that tried to run me down."

"What Jeep?"

"Parked in the church lot." He watched her steadily as he spoke, his eyes dark blue with thick, long lashes surrounding them. Women would pay to have lashes like that, and they'd probably swoon to see them on Jackson. "You know anyone with a blue Jeep?" he prodded.

"No."

"That was a quick, decisive response."

"Because I don't know anyone who owns a Jeep."

"Have you ever known anyone who did?"

"Probably, but I can't think…" Actually, she could think of someone with a blue Jeep. She and Destiny had gone to D.C. for a girls' weekend, and Destiny had borrowed her boyfriend's Jeep. "Lucas Raymond has one, but he lives in D.C."

"Lucas Raymond," he repeated. "Who's that?"

"My friend's boyfriend. I've only seen the vehicle once. I think it's newer."

"Do you have any reason to believe this guy would—"

"Raymond is a great guy. A psychiatrist. He's gotten awards for his work at the hospital and in the community."

"That doesn't mean he doesn't have an ax to grind with you." He stood and stretched, his T-shirt riding up along a firm abdomen.

She looked away, because she felt guilty noticing.

"Say we rule out Raymond," Jackson continued. "Who would want to hurt you, Raina?"

"No one," she replied, her mind working frantically, going through faces and names and situations.

"And yet, someone chased you through the woods and fired a shot at you. That same person nearly ran me down. Doesn't sound like someone who feels all warm and fuzzy when he thinks of you."

"Maybe he was a vagrant, and I scared him."

"Maybe." He didn't sound as if he believed it, and she wasn't sure she did, either.

She'd heard something that had woken her from the nightmare.

A child crying? Larry wandering around? An intruder trying to get in the house?

The last made her shudder, and she pulled her coat a little closer. "I think I'd know it if someone had a bone to pick with me."

"That's usually the case, but not always. Could be you upset a coworker or said no to a guy who wanted you to say yes."

She snorted at that, and Jackson frowned.

"You've been a widow for four years, it's not that far-fetched an idea."

"If you got a good look at my social life, you wouldn't be saying that."

Samuel yawned loudly and slid down on the pew, his arms crossed over his chest, his eyelids drooping. He looked cold and tired, and she wanted to get him home, tuck him into bed, spend a little time trying to decide how best to proceed with him.

She couldn't keep being as uncomfortable as she was, couldn't continue with her stiff and stilted approach.

"Samuel needs some medicine, and he needs some sleep," she said, taking off her coat and draping it over him.

He opened his eyes, but didn't smile.

He had the solemn look of someone much older than ten and the scars of a soldier who'd fought too many wars.

"I'll go talk to Officer Wallace," Jackson responded. "See if he's ready to let us leave."

"He's going to have to be. Samuel—"

A door slammed, the sound so startling Raina jumped.

Samuel scrambled to his feet, clutching her coat in one hand and the crutch in the other. She grabbed his shoulder, pulled him into the shelter of her arms.

"Is someone else in the church?" Jackson demanded, his gaze on the door that led from the sanctuary into the office wing.

"There shouldn't be."

"Which means whoever slammed that door doesn't belong here. Stay put. I'm going to check things out."

He strode away, and she wanted to call out and tell him to be careful. The church was cut off from the rest of River Valley, the land a couple of miles outside of town. There'd been a few break-ins during the years Matt had been pastor and several more since then.

She pressed her lips together, held in the words she knew she didn't need to say. Jackson could take care of himself. She'd seen him in action, knew just how smart and careful he was."

"I will go, too," Samuel asserted, pulling away and hopping after Jackson.

She grabbed his arm. "No, Samuel. It's not safe."

"There is nothing that is safe," he responded, and her throat burned with the reality of what he'd survived.

"You have to stay here. Let Jackson and the police take care of this. Here in the U.S., kids don't take care of adult problems." It sounded lame, but it was all she could think of.

She thought he might yank away and keep

walking, but he handed her the coat. "We will go outside, then."

"It's too cold."

"But in here it is dangerous for you. Outside, it is safe."

Maybe. Maybe not.

At this point, she didn't know, and all she could do was stay where she was and hope Jackson or Officer Andrew Wallace would figure out who was in the church or outside of it, who had been in the Jeep.

"It's safe here, Samuel. Let's just sit and wait."

He nodded but perched on the edge of the pew as if he were sure that at any moment, they'd have to run.

She waited beside him, tense, anxious, wanting to pray but unable to find the words that would spiral from her soul to God's ears.

Her faith, like so many other things in her life, was a shadow of what it had once been.

Her own fault.

After Matt and Joseph died, she'd stopped reading her Bible, stopped praying, stopped believing that God really cared. Somehow, though, He'd still rescued her from almost certain death in Africa.

There had to be a reason for that.

She'd thought it was so that she could help Samuel, but Samuel seemed perfectly capable of helping himself. Sick as he was, hurt as he was, he was ready to face the world and whatever trouble it brought him.

She wished she could say the same for herself, but the best thing she could say, the only thing that she could say, was that she was there, ready to do what God wanted.

If only she knew what that was.

# THREE

This wasn't a good time to be without a weapon, but since Officer Wallace hadn't seen fit to return Jackson's Glock, that was the situation he found himself in. He eased through the dark hall, allowing his eyes to adjust to the darkness. Straight ahead, an exit sign hung above a door. Two other doors led off the short hallway. He turned the handle of the closest one and walked into a spacious office, running his hand along the wall until he found a light switch.

A large desk took up one corner of the room, a high-back rolling chair behind it. Two other chairs stood near a wall lined with shelves and books. Another wall was blank, but for several portrait photos that must have been of former pastors and their families.

His heart did a little pause and jerk when he recognized Raina's blond hair and violet eyes. Her face had been fuller then, her cheekbones not as sharp, the area beneath less gaunt. She sat beside a dark-haired man whose smile looked genuine, and she held a little boy who looked just like his father.

Her family.

He filed the information away, turned off the light and left the room.

The next door opened just as easily, and he walked into a large choir room. Piano in one corner, racks of long blue choir robes in another. Chairs were arranged in a semicircle in front of a music stand. He stood still, listening to silence that seemed too thick and heavy to be natural.

Someone was there.

"You may as well show yourself," he said, moving toward the choir robes. "I know you're here."

Nothing, but he thought he saw a robe sway. Not much. Just a hint of movement. Enough to get his heart pumping and adrenaline coursing through him.

"I said—"

Someone lunged from the robes, darting out so quickly Jackson barely had time to respond. He dove toward the scurrying figuring, bringing the person down to the ground in a hail of fists and kicking feet. The music stand fell, clanging onto the ground with enough noise to wake the dead.

Jackson grabbed a skinny arm, tried to grab another, a man's hoarse cries filling his ears.

"Cool it!" he said as he finally managed to snag the guy's flailing hand. He looked down into a grizzled face and hot black eyes.

"Let me go, worthless VC!" the guy shouted.

"You're not in Vietnam, man," Jackson tried to assure him, still holding his arms in a tight grip. "You're in the States. In Maryland. In a church."

He was rewarded with spit in the face.

He didn't bother wiping it off.

He'd experienced worse, heard worse than the stream of curses coming from the man's mouth.

"Tell you what, buddy," he suggested, hauling the guy to his feet. "How about you put a sock in it?"

"Give me a sock and I'll—"

"What's going on?" Raina peered in the open door, her face pale. She looked like a dim reflection of the happy young woman in the photo he'd seen, and he felt exactly the way he had when he'd seen her in Africa. Worried. Determined. Willing to do whatever it took to get her home safely.

Only they weren't in Africa. They weren't even in danger. Unless a hundred-pound sixty-something-year-old man who smelled like the inside of a beer keg could be considered a threat.

"I found this guy hiding in the choir robes," he responded, turning his attention back to his prisoner, because he didn't want to look in Raina's face. He didn't want to see the loss written so clearly there, didn't want to know that her pain was the same pain he felt when he remembered Charity. Because there was nothing that could be done about that kind of pain. No magic pill that could be taken, no barrier that could be put up. Nothing but time could ease it, and even that only dulled the sharp edge of grief.

"I wasn't hiding!"

"Butch," Raina said. "You know you're not supposed to be in here without permission."

She stepped farther into the room. "Did you ask Pastor Myer if you could sleep here?"

"It's God's house. I asked *Him,*" Butch said with a sly smile.

"How about you show a little respect for the lady, Butch?" Jackson asked, giving the guy a little shake. Not too hard, though. He didn't want to rattle fragile bones.

Raina ignored his comment.

So did Butch.

As a matter of fact, Jackson thought they'd done this whole thing before—many times—and that they were just letting things play out the way they always had before.

"You've been drinking again." Raina walked

to the choir robes and dug through them, pulling out an empty bottle of beer.

"Nah. I'm just collecting old bottles for the money," Butch replied. "Gotta make a living somehow."

"You could try getting a job," Jackson muttered, releasing the guy's arms.

"Who's going to hire me? I got PTSD, a bum back, wrecked knees. Got no hearing in one ear and barely any in the other. Thank you, Uncle Sam, for taking care of your veterans." Butch grabbed a backpack from behind the clothes, not nearly as drunk as Jackson thought.

"If you need work, I have some jobs around the house that I can't do myself," Raina said casually.

Jackson doubted there was anything casual about the offer.

As a matter of fact, tension lines were etched across her forehead, her skin pulled taut along her cheekbones.

He also doubted it was a good idea to have a guy like Butch hanging around her place. He'd steal her blind and not feel a bit of guilt about it.

"What kind of jobs? 'Cause I already told you, my back is bad and my knees are gone."

"The fence needs whitewashing, and the lawn needs one more mowing before winter."

"You still got that riding lawn mower? The one Matt loved so much?"

At his question, Raina tensed, her hands fisting. "Yes."

"I'll come by day after tomorrow and get that done for you. The fence might be a little harder. Probably will take me a week or more. Gotta take lots of breaks."

Raina nodded, but didn't speak.

Jackson wasn't sure if it was the mention of her husband that had thrown her or if it was the fact that Butch had taken her up on her offer of work.

"See you then, Raina." Butch waved and would have walked out into the hall, but Jackson wasn't done with the guy.

"How long were you in here, Butch?" he asked, and the old vet paused on the threshold, his gray hair falling in a ratty braid down the middle of his back.

"Awhile," he finally muttered.

"You must have heard the gunshots earlier."

"Could be that I did." Butch turned slowly, his black eyes blazing in his gnarled face. He looked older than he probably was. Seventy or more when Jackson suspected he was in his early sixties. Life hadn't been kind to him, but then, Jackson doubted the guy had been very kind to life.

"Did you hear anything before that?" Jackson pressed.

"Who wants to know?"

"Me. Probably the police. Raina."

"Here's the deal, soldier," Butch responded. "I don't deal with the police, and I don't like you. For Raina's sake, I'll tell you this—I heard a car pull into the parking lot a couple of hours ago. You tell the police that, and I'll tell them you're lying."

"Butch—" Raina started to say, but the guy raised a hand, cutting her off.

"You've always been good to me, but I'm not getting pulled into trouble. Been there too many times to count, and I'm starting to realize I'm getting too old for it."

"You didn't just hide in the choir robes and let whoever was in the parking lot do what he wanted to the church, Butch," Jackson said. "You went and looked out a window, right? This is your space. You were ready to protect it. You looked out the window, and you saw something. It wouldn't hurt to tell the police what that was."

"Wouldn't hurt. Wouldn't help. I'm an old, drunk vet who's been wandering around these parts sleeping in churches and abandoned railroad cars and under overpasses for more years than either of you have been alive. I've got a rap sheet a mile long. You think the police would listen to a word I said? Even if they did, my word is worth squat."

"It's worth something to me," Raina cut in, and Butch frowned.

"Could be I looked. Could be I saw an old Jeep. Could even be that I saw someone get out of that Jeep and walk into the woods, but even if all those things are really what happened, ain't one person around here who's going to believe me."

"You need to tell the police what you saw," Raina suggested, and Butch scowled.

"I owe you, Raina, and I owe your husband. I even owe your little boy, but I'm not talking to the police." He hitched the pack onto his back and walked out into the hall.

Jackson could have stopped him, could have forced him outside and brought him to Officer Wallace. He didn't. Butch was obviously a well-known figure in the community. If Wallace wanted to interview him, he could track him down easily enough.

He followed Butch into the hall, watching as the guy limped to the exit, opened the door and disappeared outside. Cold air wafted in, the scent of rain and wet leaves hanging in the hallway after the door closed.

"Poor Butch," Raina murmured, her arm brushing his as she stepped past. She smelled like flowers, the scent feminine and alluring. She'd chopped her hair short, the thick strands just reaching her nape. On some women, the style would have been harsh, but on Raina it worked.

Everything about her worked.

The faded jeans and flannel nightgown. The unadorned fingernails and scuffed boots. She looked natural, and he found that beautiful, but he didn't think she saw Butch for who he was—a guy who'd take what he could, use who he could and never feel a bit of guilt over it.

"He's made his choices," Jackson responded. "Those choices brought him to the place he is."

"Maybe if he'd had a family who cared about him, he would have made different choices." She ran her fingers through her hair and sighed. "I'd better get back to Samuel. I really do want to get him home."

"Let's go, then." He cupped her elbow, as ready as she was to leave the church and get on with things. "We need to talk to Officer Wallace. Let him know what Butch saw."

"Unfortunately, he didn't see much."

"Not much that he's telling us, but he may be more open to providing details when the police bring him in for questioning."

"I really hope Andrew doesn't do that to him.

He'll probably resist and end up being arrested for it."

"Andrew?"

"Officer Wallace."

He nodded, leading her back down the hall into the sanctuary and telling himself that it wasn't his business that Raina was on a first name basis with Wallace.

*Pull away!* Raina's brain shouted as she and Jackson stepped into the quiet sanctuary, but her body refused to obey.

There was something…nice about having his hand cupped around her elbow, his fingers curved along her inner arm.

She let herself be ushered to the pew where Samuel still sat. She'd given him a pen and an old church bulletin that she'd found, and she'd told him to stay put.

He'd listened.

Thank the Lord.

She didn't think she could take any more drama. After six months of living quietly, of going to work and returning home, of going to church and returning home, of quiet dinners with friends and quiet evenings trying to forget just how alone she was, she'd stepped into a world of chaos.

All she wanted to do was step out of it again.

And not with Jackson's hand around her arm, his fingers a warm reminder of what she'd lost when Matt and Joseph had been taken away from her.

"Ready to get out of here, buddy?" Jackson asked, releasing her elbow as he took Samuel's hand and helped him to his feet.

Samuel nodded, but he seemed too tired to speak, his eyes glassy from fever.

"We'll go to the house, get some medicine in you. Maybe a little something to eat," Raina told him, her voice tighter than she wanted it to be.

"I'm not hungry," he protested weakly, but she still planned to make him some soup, maybe a piece of toast.

"You'll be hungry once that fever goes down," Jackson commented, holding the door open so they could walk outside. "You'll probably eat half the house."

"I can't eat a house," Samuel sounded more confused than amused, but he edged away from Raina and moved closer to Jackson.

She felt like a third wheel as the two discussed how much a healthy kid could eat. She tried not to let it bother her.

Rays of sunlight streamed over distant mountains and gleamed on the hood of Andrew's squad car. He waved, motioning them over. "I'm about done here. Anything else you want to add to what you told me?"

He eyed Jackson, looking as if he thought there might be more information to be had. That was the way Andrew had been for as long as Raina had known him—driven, serious and devoted to the law.

"Actually," Jackson replied, "there was someone in the church who might have seen the Jeep and its driver."

He explained briefly while Raina and Stella helped Samuel back into the SUV. Raina was about to slide in beside him when Andrew touched her shoulder.

"Hold on a second, Rain," he said quietly, and she paused, her hand on the hood of the vehicle, her back to Andrew. "I found something in the woods. I think you need to see it."

A crisp breeze blew dead leaves across the pavement. She watched as they skittered toward the SUV, refusing to turn, because she was afraid of what she'd see in Andrew's eyes.

"Rain?" he said again, and she knew she couldn't avoid it.

She turned, cold air bathing cheeks that suddenly felt too hot and too tight. "What is it?"

He hesitated. A sure sign that whatever he had to show her was as horrible as she'd thought it would be. She knew Andrew well, knew him enough to know that hesitation meant worry and worry meant things were bad.

Destiny's brother had spent most of the time Raina was growing up teasing her. After she'd married Matt, he'd stayed close, forming as strong a bond with him as he had with Raina. He'd responded to the accident that killed Matt and Joseph, and he'd been the one to tell Raina that Matt had died at the scene. He'd been at her side when the doctors declared Joseph brain-dead. He knew what she'd been through, and he'd never have wanted to add to it.

She had a feeling he was going to.

"Whatever it is, just show me," she demanded, her voice hoarse with fear.

She hated that, hated that Stella was standing on the other side of the SUV, watching with curiosity. Hated that Jackson's eyes were filled with pity.

"I left it where it was until I could bring in an evidence team, but I have a picture. I want to get your take on it." He was all business, his tone brusque just the way it usually was when he was working.

But he watched her with that steady gaze, that sorrowful look that she'd only ever seen one other time.

She didn't want to see the picture.

She didn't want to know what he'd found.

Because she was afraid that whatever it was would change everything, that it would turn her life upside down, make her question everything she believed, make her want to turn the hands of time back.

Just like four years ago.

Just like the day she'd lost everything.

Andrew reached into his pocket and pulled out a camera. He scrolled through a couple of photos and frowned. "Here it is."

She took the camera, her hands steady despite the fact that her entire body seemed to be shaking. The image on the screen was clear. Wet ground, bright-colored leaves strewn around. That wasn't the focus of the picture, though. A stuffed dog was. Fluffy and blue. About twelve inches high. Muddy and wet, but obviously well loved by a child, its ears ratty, its fur threadbare in a few places. She knew that if she could lift the dog out of the camera and study it closely, she'd be able to see that one eye was missing and that its tail had almost no fur. She thought that if she could hold it close to her nose, she'd still be able to smell baby powder and shampoo on it.

Her eyes burned, her chest so tight and heavy she didn't think she'd ever breathe again.

"It looks like the dog I gave Joseph that day we all went to the county fair together. Remember?" Andrew prodded.

Remember?

She couldn't forget. Not any second of any minute of the short time she'd had with her son. If she let herself, she'd lie in bed at night, remembering his laughter, his chubby toddler belly and happy blue eyes.

She *never* let herself.

And she didn't want this…*reminder.*

She thrust the camera back into Andrew's hands and turned on her heels, walking away from him and from Jackson. Walking past the SUV and Stella, leaving Samuel right where he was. Walking faster and faster until her feet were flying and her breath was heaving, and she was running so fast her legs ached and her lungs hurt, and the tears were streaming down her face.

And still, she couldn't outrun her sorrow.

# FOUR

Footsteps pounded behind her, but she didn't stop. She knew the way home. Just a mile to the main road, a half mile from there to the dirt road and another mile to the house. She'd run it many times in the past few years, so many times she thought she might have worn potholes into the pavement.

"You can't run forever," Jackson said, his voice and breath so even he might have been walking.

Her breathing was frantic, her lungs burning from cold air, from anger, from sorrow, from all the emotions that stuffed dog had made her feel.

It couldn't be Joseph's.

Could it?

Jackson grabbed her hand, forcing her to slow down to a walk. She could have pulled away. His grip was loose, his touch light.

She let her hand lie where it was, the warmth

of his palm seeping into her cold skin. He didn't speak again, and she didn't.

Ahead, the sun peeked over the trees, bright gold rimmed with pink. The beginning of a new day, and she had another little boy to take care of. One who hadn't ever had a blue stuffed dog won at a local fair. Her breath caught, the tears that had been sliding down her face pooling in her throat and chest and heart.

An SUV pulled up beside them, and Jackson opened the back door. Raina slid into place beside Samuel, turning her face away because she didn't want him to know she'd been crying. He'd seen too much sorrow in his life. She didn't want to bring any more into it. She'd brought him to the United States because he'd needed more medical help than he'd been getting. She didn't want to add to his burdens or create more trouble for him.

To her surprise, he reached for her hand, his fingers hot from fever as he patted her knuckles. He didn't speak, and she couldn't speak.

"Officer Wallace said he's going to stop by your place after the evidence team arrives at the scene." Stella broke the silence, not a hint of sympathy in her voice. "I told him I'd give you the message. Here's one from me. The next time you want to go running off, don't."

"I apologize. I shouldn't have left you with Samuel," she managed to say.

"You think that's what this is about?" Stella glared into the rearview mirror. "Me not wanting to babysit the kid? I've got news for you, sister. Someone was in the woods with you this morning. That person fired a shot that could have taken you out like that." She snapped her fingers.

"He's long gone," Raina pointed out, tears drying on her cheeks, some of the shock of seeing the stuffed dog fading away.

Maybe that's what Stella had hoped for.

"You can't know that. The woods are pretty dense, and it would be easy for someone to hide in them," Stella pointed out.

"Jackson saw him drive away." And Raina couldn't imagine that the guy would have wanted to hang around. Not with the police there.

"In a Jeep with a flat tire," Jackson broke in. "He might have pulled off the road and run into the woods. Anything is possible, Raina, and Stella is right, you need to be more careful."

If she hadn't seen the photo of the stuffed dog, she might have argued that the man in the woods had been a random stranger, someone who'd been as surprised by her as she had been by him, but the dog…

Thinking about it made her stomach churn

and her throat ache. Had the dog been left there for her to find?

If so, by whom?

And why?

"The dog was your son's," Jackson said. Not a question, but she nodded anyway. "When was the last time you saw it?"

"A few weeks ago." Destiny had helped her clean out Joseph's room. They'd packed up all the things that had been sitting in the closet and the toy chest—little boy things that needed to be replaced with things a ten-year-old would enjoy.

She'd felt ready to let go of the clothes and all the stuffed animals Joseph had loved so much, but it had still been difficult. Without Destiny's prodding, she wasn't sure she could have done it. "My friend and I cleaned out Joseph's room. The dog was with the things we packed up."

"What did you do with it?"

"My friend took it to Goodwill. I had to work." And she hadn't had the heart to put the boxes of Joseph's things in her car and drive away with them.

"You're sure she took the dog to Goodwill?" Stella asked as they turned onto the dirt road that led to Raina's house.

"Yes. There were several boxes, and she took them all."

"Do you think it's possible your friend took

the dog? Maybe as a keepsake? Something to remember your son by?"

"I don't know why she would have. If she did, she wouldn't have left it in the woods."

"You're sure about that?" Stella pulled into the driveway and turned to look over the seat. "People often do unexpected things."

"Not Destiny. She's as dependable as sunrise."

"That's what everyone says right around the time they find out their best friend or sister or husband—"

"Stella," Jackson interrupted. "How about we let the police figure things out?"

"Because your brother won't like it if we butt our noses in?"

"Because you're tired, and it's starting to show."

"What are you talking about? Since when do I ever act tired?" she demanded.

Raina got out of the SUV. Let the two of them argue about what the police should handle or not. She needed to get Samuel inside, give him something for his fever, feed him.

"Come on, Samuel," she said, offering her hand. "We're home."

"This is not home," he responded, but he allowed himself to be helped out of the car. She handed him his crutch, would have ushered him into the house, but Jackson got out of the SUV.

"I'll get his bag and walk the two of you in. I want to check the house. Make sure it's clear before we leave."

"There's no need."

"I think there is, Raina," he responded, his eyes the deep dark blue of the evening sky. She could lose herself in eyes like his, so she looked away, concentrating on the ground, on Samuel's threadbare shoes, on her own scuffed boots.

"You don't really think someone is waiting in my house, do you?" she asked.

"Probably not." Stella got out of the SUV and stretched. There were dark shadows beneath her eyes, and her clothes hung limp and wrinkled from her thin frame. She'd been traveling for nearly two days, and it showed. "But better safe than sorry. Besides, I'm in desperate need of a cup of coffee. I drove all the way from Atlanta. Much as I hate to admit that Jackson is right, I'm wrung out. A little caffeine before we head back to D.C. wouldn't be a bad thing."

"I should have thought of that," Raina admitted. "Come on in. I'll start coffee and make everyone some breakfast."

"What kind of breakfast?" Stella asked.

"Bacon? Eggs? Pancakes?"

"You're speaking my language, sister. Let's go." She hooked her arm through Raina's and dragged her toward the house.

Jackson watched them go.

He had to give Stella credit. She knew how to get what the team wanted. Whether it was a helicopter in a third world country, last minute hotel accommodations in Paris or an invitation into the home of a woman who didn't seem to think she needed protection, she managed it.

He grabbed Samuel's beat-up backpack from the SUV. No suitcase. No electronic devices. No toys. Just the one bag that probably contained everything Samuel had ever owned.

The morning had gone quiet, the sun cresting the trees and shimmering in the pristine sky. Across the street, an old house jutted up from a sparse brown yard. There were no other neighbors. Whoever had been stalking Raina through the woods would have little to deter him if he decided to break into her house.

He carried Samuel's backpack up the porch steps, scanning the front yard as he went. It was a nice piece of property set on a pretty lot. He imagined Raina and her husband had been thinking that when they'd bought it, and he couldn't help wondering what Raina thought about it now.

Jackson had read the newspaper articles. He knew that Pastor Matt Lowery had been driving his son to get ice cream when he'd plunged over an embankment. He'd been killed instantly.

Raina's son had survived for three days before succumbing to his injuries.

It couldn't be easy to live in the house they'd all shared.

He knocked, then opened the door and stepped inside. The place was homey, the living room furnished with a sturdy couch and love seat, two end tables and a coffee table. A large fireplace took up most of one wall, a watercolor painting hanging above it.

Someone had painted the walls a cheery yellow and hung flowery curtains from the windows. The place wasn't cheery, though. It had the empty stagnant feel of museum air. He knew how that happened, knew what it was like when a member of a family suddenly wasn't there. His parents had tried to fill the space Charity had left, but they'd never been able to. Eventually, they'd sold the house Jackson had been raised in, downsizing to a little cottage on a couple of acres.

He followed the sound of voices through the living room and into a dining room. A doorway opened from there into the kitchen. Spacious and gleaming, it felt warmer than the other rooms. A small square table stood against one wall, the Formica top nicked with age and use. Stella sat in a chair there, a cup of coffee in her hands, exhaustion etching fine lines near the corners of her eyes. Samuel leaned against the counter, his crutch forgotten on the floor beside him. Like Stella, he looked exhausted, his eyes tracking Raina's movements as she cracked eggs into a skillet.

"There's coffee in the pot. Mugs in the cupboard next to the sink. Go ahead and pour yourself some," Raina said, glancing over her shoulder and offering a smile. "If you take cream, it's in the fridge. Sugar in that little jar on the table."

"Thanks." He grabbed a mug, poured the coffee. No cream or sugar. Just black. He needed it as much as Stella seemed to. He'd been pushing hard for the past few months, running mission after mission. If he hadn't nearly gotten himself killed in Egypt, he'd probably still be running.

"Want some help with the food?" he asked.

"No. Thanks." She turned back to the eggs, her shoulders tense, her hand shaking as she cracked another one into the skillet.

"I'm thinking you do." He leaned over her shoulder, picked a piece of shell from the pan. "Otherwise, we'll all be eating crunchy scrambled eggs."

"You cook it, and we'll be eating burnt eggs," Stella muttered.

"I don't burn food," he protested, the scent of flowers and sunshine filling his nose. At first he thought the window was open and a spring breeze was wafting in. But it wasn't spring, and the air outside was cool and moist.

Raina shifted, her hair brushing his chin, and the scents floated in the air again. Flowers. Sunshine.

"Nice shampoo," he murmured without thinking, and Raina's cheeks went three shades of red.

She ducked away, hurrying to a bright yellow refrigerator that looked as if it had been there since the 1940s. "I have bacon and sausage. Which do you prefer?"

He wasn't sure who she was asking, but Stella shook her head. "No bacon. No sausage. Not for me, anyway. And I don't think for Samuel. He looks like he's about to fall over."

"He needs to get some sleep, but I want him to eat first." Raina spooned eggs onto a plate, dropped a slice of toast onto it and set it on the table. "There you go, Samuel."

"I'm not hungry." But Samuel sat down anyway, accepting the fork that Raina handed him and digging into the food.

Hungry or not, it seemed he was going to eat.

Stella, on the other hand, shook her head when Raina offered her a plate. "I'm too tired to eat. I don't even think the coffee is going to wake me up."

"I have a couple of spare rooms," Raina said

as she scooped more eggs onto the plate. "You're welcome to use one."

"If the room in question has a bed, I'm there."

"It does." Raina buttered a second piece of toast, spread jam on top of it and set it next to the eggs. She handed the plate to Jackson, and unlike Stella, he wasn't too tired to eat.

"Thanks."

"There's no need for thanks," Raina said. "A couple of eggs and two slices of toast doesn't even come close to repaying you for what you did in Africa."

"We got paid well for that gig. You don't have to feed the guy to thank him." Stella scowled.

"Hey," Jackson protested, digging into the eggs. "If she wants to cook, let her cook."

"She doesn't. She's just doing it because she feels sorry for you."

"Why," Jackson asked, knowing he was going to regret it, "would she feel sorry for me?"

"Because you're scrawny and look like a stiff breeze could blow you over. Your own fault. If you hadn't gone and gotten yourself—"

"How about you be quiet and let me enjoy my food," he growled. The last thing he wanted to do was discuss Egypt and the mistake he'd made there. It had nearly cost him his life. Something that Chance had mentioned dozens of times since Jackson had returned home with thirty stitches in his side.

"Why? Because you don't want me to embarrass you in front of a pretty young woman?" Stella smirked.

"This isn't junior high, Stel," he said mildly. "I'm not worried about being embarrassed in front of a beautiful woman."

"I said pretty. Guess you get an upgrade, Raina," Stella quipped.

Raina didn't look amused.

She looked appalled, her cheeks blazing. "I... think I'll go change the sheets on the beds in the spare rooms."

She sprinted into a small alcove and up stairs that creaked and groaned beneath her feet.

"Not cool, Stella," he chided.

Stella didn't look at all contrite. "Sure it was. I wanted her out of here, and I got my way."

"You could have just asked for privacy."

"Probably, but I'm used to working in more subtle ways." She rubbed the back of her neck and yawned. "What do you think, Jack? Are we going to be here more than a few hours?"

"Why are you asking?"

"Nothing that needs immediate discussion."

"Then why ask at all?"

"Because a girl likes to know what she's got on her agenda. If we're staying until we take a nap and regain some pep, that's one thing. If we stay for a couple of days—" she shrugged "—I need to rearrange my schedule."

"You don't have any missions. Not for the next week or two." Like Jackson, Stella was going on a forced vacation. Chance's idea. He'd insisted they both needed time to renew.

He was probably right, but it wasn't something Jackson planned to admit. Not to his brother, anyway.

"What's your point, Jack?"

"That your schedule is probably as empty as mine is."

"You're assuming that I don't have a social life, and you're assuming wrong." She tossed nonexistent locks of hair over her shoulder and probably would have made a show of marching from the room, but her gaze dropped to Samuel.

He'd managed to eat half the eggs and a few bites of toast, but his head was drooping. His eyes closed.

"He's about to face-plant in the eggs," she commented. "You keep him from doing that, and I'll go ask Raina where he's going to be sleeping."

She left the room but didn't head upstairs.

Apparently, she had something else to do. A phone call to make? He could hear her talking to someone, and he was curious to know who.

Every member of HEART was family, and in his family, one person's business was every person's business.

He'd have followed her, gotten close enough to eavesdrop, if he hadn't had Samuel to contend with. The kid was drifting off again, his head dropping closer to the plate and the eggs that were still on it.

He eased the boy up, pressed the fork back into his hand.

"You need to eat more," he encouraged, his head cocked to the side as he strained to hear what Stella was saying.

No luck with that. The walls of the old house were thick and he couldn't hear anything but faint mumblings and the soft creak of the floor above his head.

"I've been had, Samuel," he said, dropping into the chair beside the young boy.

Samuel nodded, his eyes glassy and vague.

"Stella is a wily one," he continued, hoping to keep Samuel awake.

"What is wily?" Samuel mumbled through a mouthful of eggs.

"Smart. Sneaky."

Samuel shrugged, his eyelids drooping as he shoved another bite of eggs into his mouth. "I like Stella."

"Everyone likes Stella, but that doesn't mean she's not a manipulative piece of work."

"Mmm-hmm," Samuel responded, and then the fork dropped from his hand, his eyes closed and Jackson just managed to catch him before the face-plant Stella had predicted came true.

# FIVE

An hour later, and everyone had been tucked away into his or her own bedroom. Jackson knew he should try to sleep, but he felt wound-up and on edge. Too much coffee and too many eggs. Not to mention the third piece of toast Raina had made him after she'd gotten Samuel into bed.

Homemade bread and homemade raspberry jam. Breakfast had been the best he'd eaten in months. Maybe even years. That didn't say much about the quality of Jackson's culinary skills. Not that he spent all that much time in his D.C. apartment. When he was there, he didn't cook. He ate out. Sometimes alone, sometimes with one of his siblings. Sometimes with a date.

Dates had been few and far between lately. He'd been too busy. Always busy. That's what his sister Trinity said. Of course, she'd been try-ing to get him to take some time off work so that she could step into the company as a search-and-rescue team member, rather than as office help.

Wasn't going to happen. Not in Jackson's lifetime, anyway. He'd already lost his older sister. He had no intention of losing his younger one.

He rubbed the back of his neck and glanced around the small room Raina had escorted him to. Stella's was across a narrow hall. She'd closed the door the minute she'd stepped inside it. Unless he missed his guess, she was already in bed.

His cell phone rang, but he ignored it. Chance was the only one who'd be calling at six in the morning, and Jackson wasn't in the mood for another lecture. He kicked off his shoes and stretched out on the narrow twin bed. Not the most comfortable sleeping arrangement for a six-two, one-hundred-ninety-pound guy, but he'd slept on a lot worse.

The house settled around him, sunlight glimmering at the edges of the thick shade that covered the room's lone window. A few creaks and groans of old wood joists and Raina's house drifted into silence. He tried to let himself drift along with it, but he was wound up tight, thoughts of his run through the woods filling his head. He could picture the Jeep clearly, but he couldn't change the fact that he hadn't seen the driver.

He wanted another chance at it, but he had

a feeling the cops were going to find the Jeep abandoned somewhere, the driver long gone. If they were fortunate, there'd be evidence to lead them to the perpetrator. If not, the guy who'd stalked Raina through the woods might return to continue whatever game he'd been playing.

And Jackson had no doubt it had been a game.

The woods were thick enough and far enough from help that Raina had made an easy target. If the perp had wanted to kill her, he could have done so. Easily. The thought didn't sit well, and Jackson got up, walking to the window and opening the shade.

He had a perfect view of the front yard and the road that wound close to the property. Beyond it was the neighbor's house and beyond that thick woods stretched along a bluff. The church had to be at the top of the rise. He couldn't see it from the house, but he figured it was an easy mile and a half walk through the woods. Probably on the path he'd found.

A noise drifted into the quiet—water running, the soft clank of dishes. He didn't think about what he was doing or why, just opened the door and walked to what had probably once been servants' stairs. The walls were covered with peeling flowered paper. Raina had apologized as she'd led the way to the attic, but Jackson had seen nothing worth apologizing for. The old house had character and charm. Unlike his modern D.C. apartment, it was filled with the stories that had been lived out in it. A little dust, a little peeling wallpaper, those things were to be expected.

He walked down the stairs, wincing as they creaked. The water was still running as he walked into the kitchen. Raina stood with her back to the stairwell, her hands deep in a suds-filled sink.

"Want some help?" he asked.

She jumped and spun toward him, suds flying across the room and splattering his shirt and face.

"Oh, my gosh! I'm so sorry!" She hurried toward him, swiping at his face and shirt with a dish towel. "I didn't hear you coming."

The scent of flowers and sunshine drifted in the air, her soft hair tickling his chin the same way it had done before. His stomach clenched, every nerve in his body jumping to life. Maybe Trinity was right. Maybe his life had become too busy, his schedule too limited by endless missions. Based on his reaction to Raina, he'd say he needed to get out more, spend a few pleasant evenings with a pleasant woman.

One who did not look as though she was going to break if Jackson wasn't careful with her.

"It's okay," he muttered, taking the cloth from

Raina's hand and putting a few feet of distance between them. "I've been covered with worse."

"Still...dirty dish water?" She shook her head, her cheeks pink, a smile hovering at the corner of her lips. It changed her face, turned all the angles soft, filled in the hollows beneath her cheeks. Made her look like the woman he'd seen in the photo at the church. Young and happy and filled with enthusiasm for life.

She was beautiful. More so than she probably knew.

And he probably shouldn't be noticing, but he was.

"It's better than mud. Or spit." He handed back the dishcloth. "I've had those and a few other things that I won't mention splattered on my face."

"Maybe I should send you home with a backpack full of dishcloths," she joked, turning back to the sink and plunging her hands back into the water. She'd changed into a soft black T-shirt and faded blue sweatpants that were baggy enough and long enough to have been her husband's.

"And, maybe, *you* should sit down and take a breather. I'll take over."

"Washing dishes isn't the kind of job a person needs a breather from, but if you want..." She dug a clean cloth from a drawer and handed it to him. "You can dry. The plates go in the cupboard to the left of the stove. Utensils—"

"In the drawer beneath it?"

"Yes." She didn't look up from the pan she was scrubbing. Jackson had the distinct impression that she wasn't comfortable having him beside her, but she didn't comment further as he lifted a bright yellow plate from the drainer and dried it.

If she'd had her way, they probably would have finished the job in silence, but Jackson had some questions he wanted to ask, some things he needed to know. In a few hours, he and Stella would head back to D.C., and Raina and Samuel would be on their own, sitting ducks in Raina's little house in the middle of the woods.

He frowned, sliding the plate into the cupboard and grabbing another. "You've got a pretty piece of property out here, Raina," he commented, hoping to open up the line of communication, maybe make her a little more comfortable.

"You mean secluded?" She met his eyes. "That's what Matt liked about it."

"Matt was your husband?"

"I think you know he was."

He didn't deny it, and she sighed, grabbing a couple of mugs from a cupboard and filling both with coffee. She didn't offer, just handed him the cup and then sat at the table. "We're probably both going to need more caffeine for this conversation."

"I'm already pretty wired, but thanks." He set the cup on the counter and dried a small handful of utensils.

"Do you like the seclusion?" he asked, eying the backyard beyond the kitchen window. He could imagine living in a place like this one. Set apart from the hectic pace of D.C., it seemed like exactly the sort of place he'd want to raise a family in. If he were going to have a family.

Right now, that was off the table.

He didn't have the time. His relationship with Amanda had proven that. If she hadn't broken things off three months before their wedding, they'd be living unhappily ever after, her constant frustration with his travel stealing any joy they might have found when he was home.

"Sometimes," she responded. "Other times, it's lonely."

"Have you considered moving?"

"Yes. Hundreds of times."

"But you're still here," he pointed out, carrying his mug to the table and taking the seat beside her.

"Selling a property that's out in the middle of nowhere isn't as easy as buying one. Even if it were, I'm still not sure I'm ready to leave.

There are a lot of memories here." She fingered a scratch in the Formica. "I'd feel like I was letting those go if I walked away." She dug at the scratch, her short fingernail bending. In another minute, it would rip, but she didn't seem to care.

He covered her hand, gently stopping its movements.

She stiffened, looked straight into his eyes. "What?" she asked as if he had said something.

"The memories aren't in the place."

"That's easy to say, Jackson. If you've never lost someone you loved."

"You're making assumptions, Raina. That's never a good thing."

"I'm just stating a fact. Unless a person has experienced what I have—"

"My sister was kidnapped in Cambodia eight years ago," he cut her off. "She hasn't been recovered. My folks sold the house we all grew up in because they couldn't stand to live in it after she was gone. That didn't help ease their grief. Every Christmas they buy her a gift and put it in their spare bedroom. They do the same on her birthday. You can't walk in that room without seeing what was lost or feeling every memory they have of her."

"I'm sorry," Raina said, turning her hand so that she could squeeze Jackson's. She'd been washing dishes, feeling sorry for herself, and she'd allowed that to color their conversation.

"For what?" he asked, his fingers twining through hers, his skin rough and warm. Her heart ached at the contact, all the memories she'd been reliving as she'd stared out into the backyard fading as she looked into his dark blue eyes.

"For what happened to your sister. And for making assumptions. You're right. That's never a good idea." She eased her hand from his, grabbed cream from the fridge. She didn't need it, but she poured some into her coffee. Anything to keep from looking into his eyes again.

"You're forgiven," he responded, that deep Southern drawl as warm as his hand had been.

She shivered, staring into the coffee cup as if it could offer some answer to the reason why her heart was galloping in her chest.

"Cold?" he asked.

*Scared,* she wanted to respond.

*Of you and the way you make me feel.*

"No. Just…tired. It was a long night."

"A long six months, I'd say," he commented. "It was quite a fight to get Samuel here."

"That's true, but it will be worth it if he regains his health. This is the best place for him to do that."

"I'm glad you think so. There are plenty of

people who would have sent money for his care and left him right where he was."

"He'd have died there, Jackson. I couldn't live with that. Although, right at this moment, I think he'd be happier if I could have."

Much happier.

Samuel hadn't said a word to her when she'd brought him to his room, had seemed angry when she'd tried to help him into cotton pajamas. He'd brushed her hands away, turned his back to her. She'd been too tired to respond with anything other than "Sleep well."

"He's sick and exhausted and probably a good bit of scared. Don't base your judgment of how this year is going to play out on today or even tomorrow."

"I'm not," she said. "I won't."

But she couldn't say it hadn't bothered her.

She'd given him Joseph's room, and she'd wanted him to feel at home in it. Otherwise, what was the point of cleaning out the drawers and the closet, packing up the boxes, moving out all of the things that had once belonged to her son?

"Andrew never showed up," she commented, wanting to change the subject and her focus. "I wonder if the evidence team found something else."

"I was wondering the same. I'm hoping

they've got the Jeep. That seems to be the key to finding our perpetrator." He took a sip of coffee, eying her over the rim of the mug. "Have you spent any time thinking about what I said?"

"You've said a lot, Jackson. Exactly what should I be thinking about?"

He chuckled, setting the mug on the counter and unwrapping the loaf of bread she'd made the previous day. She'd cut it into thin slices, and he took one, opened the fridge and grabbed the raspberry jam. "I guess I need to be more clear," he responded as he slathered the bread with jam. "Have you thought of anyone who might have a bone to pick with you? Anyone who might think it's funny to scare you?"

"Like I told you, there's no one."

"There's someone, Raina, and he definitely wanted you to know about him.

"I know." How could she not? She'd seen the guy standing in the trees, his face hidden, his eyes glittering. She shuddered, swiping sweaty palms across the sweats she'd saved when she'd cleaned out Matt's drawers and given away his clothes. They were old and worn, the fabric soft with time. She should have thrown them out, but she just kept washing them and shoving them back in her pajama drawer.

"Then maybe you can spend a little more time trying to figure out who it might be," he suggested. He bit into the bread, closed his eyes. "This is the best jam I've ever had, but if you tell Grandma Ruth I said it, I'll deny every word."

"Are you afraid she'll disown you?"

"I'm afraid she'll smack me upside the head with her frypan."

The comment surprised a laugh out of her.

"That's better," he said, running a knuckle along her cheek.

Her breath caught, her heart jerking hard. "What?"

"You laughing. You should do it more often, Raina. It's good for the soul."

"What I should probably do is get some rest," she responded, moving away because standing close to Jackson wasn't conducive to clear thinking. "As soon as Samuel wakes up, I'm taking him to the clinic. He has an infection that needs to be treated."

"That's what Stella said," he replied before she could make an excuse and leave the kitchen. She wanted to go, because the last time she'd been in the kitchen alone with a man, the man had been Matt.

"She's a nurse, right?" That's what Raina had been told when she'd contacted HEART and asked if someone there would be willing to escort Samuel to the United States. Two days later, she'd gotten a call from the owner and CEO,

Chance Miller. He'd said they'd be happy to help and that they had a nurse on staff who'd be perfect for the job.

Raina hadn't realized the nurse was the woman she'd met in Africa until a few weeks later.

Not that it would have mattered.

She hadn't wanted Samuel to travel alone. Even if she had, the airline wouldn't allow it. He was still sick, still fragile, and *she* was too much of a chicken to step foot on African soil again. Hiring someone was the only option, and the people at HEART already knew the situation, knew Samuel, knew what he'd been through and what he needed.

"She was a navy nurse for a few years before she joined the team." Jackson replied. "You two probably have a lot in common."

"I doubt it. I've spent most of my life in River Valley." Except for college and the mission trip to Kenya, she'd never considered going anywhere else.

"You were an emergency room nurse here," he pointed out.

"I was. Now I work at Moreland Medical Center."

"Owned by Dr. Kent Moreland, right? He spearheaded the mission team you were part of in Kenya."

"You know a lot more about my life than I

know about yours. I'm not very comfortable with that." She leaned her hip against the counter, looked straight into his face. He needed to shave. Or maybe not. The stubble on his jaw added to his rugged good looks.

She blushed, but didn't shift her gaze.

"Ask me any question you want to about my life, and I'll answer," he offered, not even a hint of humor in his eyes.

"Why are you here? I thought Stella was escorting Samuel alone," she asked, because she didn't want to ask him anything personal. She didn't want to know if he had a wife, kids, a family that was waiting for him when he returned home.

Or maybe she did and just didn't want to admit it to herself.

He raised an eyebrow. "Playing chicken, Raina?"

"What's that supposed to mean?"

"That you could have asked me anything, and that's a pretty lame choice."

"Okay. Fine. What is your family like?"

"Big. I have three brothers and two sisters. One of them is missing, but I already told you about that."

"Is that why you and your brother founded HEART?"

"That would be exactly why." He moved close,

his broad shoulders blocking her view of the room, his gaze steady. "Now it's my turn."

"I didn't know we were taking turns."

"You do now." He tucked a strand of hair behind her ear, his fingers trailing along her jaw. "It's been four years since your husband died. Why are you still wearing his sweats?"

The question jolted her from the moment, from whatever strange spell Jackson was weaving. "That's a really personal question."

"I thought the rule was that we could ask anything."

"No rules, because this isn't a game," she snapped, more embarrassed than angry. It had been four years, and that did seem like a long time to be wearing her deceased husband's sweats. "But I'll answer your question, and then I'm going to my room to get some rest. I'm wearing the sweats because they're comfortable and because they remind me of Matt. If that's a crime—"

"I don't recall saying that it was," he cut in gently. "I was just curious."

"Why?"

"Because I want to know just how in love with your husband you still are, Raina."

"I—"

The doorbell rang, cutting off whatever response she might have given. It was for the best.

She had no idea what she would have said, no answer that really made sense. She loved Matt, but she wasn't in love with him. Not anymore. She was more in love with the idea of what they'd still have if he hadn't been taken from her.

She ran to the door, her heart pounding hollowly in her chest. She shouldn't care about Jackson's reasons for asking such a personal question. She shouldn't wonder why he had.

Somehow, though, she did.

# SIX

Jackson followed Raina from the kitchen, sticking close as she hurried to the front door. It was early for a visitor. At least in Jackson's world it was. Raina didn't seem bothered by it. She peered through the peephole, her husband's sweats skimming over narrow hips and thin legs. He shouldn't have asked about the pants, but he'd wanted to know. He'd spent the past six months trying to get Raina out of his head. He'd failed. He was still trying to figure out why. He'd blame that on his lapse of judgment and forget about the way his heart softened every time he looked into her violet eyes.

"Kent!" Raina exclaimed, unlocking the door and pulling it open. "What are you doing here?"

"Since you wouldn't let me come to the airport with you, I spent half the night awake, worrying about Samuel." A tall, lanky man stepped into the house, his dark slacks and white dress shirt perfectly pressed, his shoes polished to a high gleam. Jackson had seen him before in much worse circumstances—a few weeks' worth of beard on his emaciated face, his eyes burning bright with fever. Dr. Kent Moreland had recovered well from his time in the Sudanese insurgent camp, his face filling out, his smooth-shaven jaw and cheeks nicely tanned. He looked as though he spent a fair amount of time in the gym and probably even more on the golf course. Not that it was any of Jackson's business or concern.

"I didn't go to the airport, either, so you didn't miss out on much," Raina responded, brushing a hand over her T-shirt and sweats.

"No?" Kent's gaze jumped to Jackson, and he frowned. "I didn't realize you had a guest. I guess that's his SUV parked in your driveway?"

"I have guests. This is Jackson Miller from HEART. He and his coworker brought Samuel here. The ice storm delayed the flight, so they drove," Raina offered. If she felt uncomfortable, it didn't show.

The doctor, on the other hand, looked fit to be tied, his dark eyes flashing with what could have been irritation, judgment or both.

"I see," Kent said. "I wish I would have known that. I'd have come by earlier."

"It's already pretty early," Jackson pointed out.

Kent eyed him for a moment, his gaze hard.

Jackson thought he'd say something sarcastic. Instead, his expression changed, the irritation in his eyes fading away.

"True." He smiled. "I was on my way to work. Sometimes I forget the rest of the world isn't filled with morning people. I'm Dr. Kent Moreland."

He offered a hand, and Jackson clasped it, not convinced that the change in attitude was sincere. "I remember. We met on a helicopter about six months ago."

Kent stilled, his dark brown eyes settling more intently on Jackson's face. "You were in Africa?"

"Yes."

"I wish I could say *I* remember *you*. When it comes to my time in Africa, things are a little fuzzy around the edges." He sat on the couch, his legs stretched out and crossed at the ankles, his muscles relaxed. From the look of things, he'd been there dozens of times before. Something about that bothered Jackson, but he refused to acknowledge the reason.

"I'm not surprised. You were out of it when we found you," he offered, and Kent nodded.

"I'd say I was within twenty-four hours of dying when your team arrived. I owe you guys a lot."

"We were paid for what we did," he responded. It sounded cold. He didn't mean it to.

The fact was, HEART took on clients who could pay and those who could not. Cases were decided on an individual basis, discussed as a team and agreed on as a team. Money was never the biggest factor to consider. Family was. If HEART could bring someone home, reunite loved ones, make one less person suffer loss… they'd do it. No matter what the cost.

"I know, but I'm still grateful. If not for HEART, Raina and I would have ended up like the rest of the mission team."

*Dead, you mean?* Jackson wanted to ask, because Kent seemed almost too nonchalant about what had happened to the other doctors and nurses.

Eight people gone, their lives ended by men who valued nothing but their own agenda. Did the doctor feel any sorrow over that or was he just relieved to be one of the survivors?

That was a question Jackson would never ask, but he was thinking it as Raina settled onto the edge of the love seat and smiled in his direction.

That smile did something to him. Made his heart jerk to attention, reminded him that being a bachelor hadn't always been part of his life plan.

"Kent is right. I think with all the excitement of last night, I forgot to tell you and Stella how thankful I am for what HEART did," she said quietly. There was no mistaking the sincerity in her voice or the sorrow in her eyes. She felt the loss. Even if Kent didn't.

Jackson felt it, too. HEART had hoped to bring everyone out of the insurgent camp alive. They hadn't been able to, but at least the families who'd been waiting and praying and hoping had closure. He tried to take comfort in that.

"I wish we could have done more," he responded honestly.

"From the reports I've read, everyone else on the team had been dead for at least twenty-four hours before you arrived. There was nothing you could have done for them," Kent said, his eyes on Raina, a frown line carved deep between his brows. "What kind of excitement did you have last night?"

"Excitement might have been an overstatement. It was just a little…drama."

"With Samuel? I was worried that would happen. He lived most of his life as a child soldier, and there's no way—"

"No, not with Samuel," Raina cut him off. "Someone was hanging around outside my house before Samuel got here. I had to call the police."

She didn't mention her run through the woods or the shots that had been fired at her.

"Who was it?" Kent demanded.

"I don't know, but the police are going to try to find out."

"They better find out soon," Kent muttered. "I've never liked the idea of you being out here alone. Now I like it even less. Maybe you should move into town. I have that rental property on Main Street. You and Samuel could stay there."

"I appreciate the offer, Kent, but I'll be fine."

"It's not just you anymore, Raina. It's a ten-year-old boy who's been through the wringer. He needs stability and security. Not excitement and danger."

"He needs to get well, and he will," Raina responded.

"Not if some creep breaks into your place and—"

"No one is going to break in," Raina assured him. "The police have a witness and they should be able to find the guy quickly. In the meantime, I'll keep the windows locked and the door bolted."

"A witness? Your neighbor, you mean? Because you said Luke's memory seems to be going. I doubt he'll be able to give the police many details."

"His name is Larry. Not Luke," Raina said. "And he's not the witness. Bu—"

"Raina." Jackson put a hand on her shoulder.

"I'm not sure the police would want that information to be public."

Kent frowned. "No worries, Jackson. I'm not going to tell anyone."

"I'm sure you won't, but I think we should let the police decide whether or not the information should be given out." Besides, he was getting a little tired of the doctor, and he was ready to send him on his way.

"I can probably guess," Kent persisted. "There's only one person I know of who wanders around near here. Butch Hendricks? Seeing as how he's usually drunk as a skunk, I don't think his testimony will hold much weight."

"Maybe not. You can ask Andrew Wallace about it, if you want to. He was the responding officer."

"I think I will. I saw him on my way here. He and a couple of other officers were taking photos of an old Jeep that was stuck on the side of the road."

Jackson's pulse leaped at the words. "What color was the Jeep?"

"Blue? Black? I think it had been in an accident. One of the tires was flat as a pancake and the front was dented."

"Where did you see them?" Raina asked, her gaze on Jackson. He could see hope blazing from the depth of her gaze, and he wanted to tell her not to get too excited. Finding the Jeep didn't mean finding the perpetrator. It was a start, though, and that was something to be thankful for.

"Three miles away from here. On Highway 6."

"That's the local road that runs between here and town," Raina explained, and Jackson nodded.

"What?" Kent glanced from one to the other, his gaze settling on Jackson. "Is there something I should know?"

"Ask Officer Wallace. He'll give you whatever information he thinks is necessary." From Jackson's past experience dealing with law enforcement, he'd guess that would be next to nothing.

He kept that thought to himself as Raina stood, smoothing her T-shirt. "You'd probably better do that after your workday ends, Kent. Speaking of which, if you don't leave now, you'll be late."

"Are you kicking me out, Raina?" Kent teased. "Because something like that could really hurt a guy's feelings."

"I'm not kicking you out. I'm kicking you to your office, because I have to get some rest before I bring Samuel to see you," she responded lightly, pulling the door open and ushering Kent outside.

Jackson followed. Mostly because he was curious about the two of them. Were they a couple? Raina didn't seem to think so, but Jackson had the distinct impression that the doctor felt differently.

"My schedule is full, but I'll clear a spot for him. Just call when you're on your way."

"I appreciate it, Kent."

"It's my pleasure." He dropped a hand to her shoulder and smiled. "We made it through worse together. We'll make it through this."

*Together?*

Obviously, the doctor had a major thing for Raina.

Did she know it?

Jackson watched as she slid away from Kent's hand, crossed her arms over her chest. Not the body language of someone who felt comfortable and at ease with a situation. "Samuel will be fine. Thanks for stopping by, Kent. I'll see you in a couple of hours."

"See you in a few hours," Kent called as he walked down the porch steps.

Raina wanted to walk back inside and close the door, but she didn't want to be rude. Good manners had been bred into her, and she waited on the porch, waving as Kent got into his Corvette.

Jackson stood beside her, and she tried not to

notice the warmth of his arm pressed close to hers or the way the sunlight added fiery strands to his dark hair. She tried not to think about the question he'd asked or about the way he'd looked when he'd said he wanted to know if she was still in love with Matt.

"So," he asked as Kent pulled away, "want to tell me about you and the good doctor?"

"There's nothing to tell," she responded truthfully.

"Does he know that?" Jackson slid an arm around her waist and led her back into the house.

"Of course he does," she responded, stepping away from his warmth and almost wishing that she didn't have to. It had been a long time since a man had put his arm around her waist. A long time since she'd wanted one to.

She wasn't sure what to think about that, and she was too tired to figure it out.

"You're sure?"

"I work for him, Jackson. There's no way we could have a relationship. Even if one of us wanted to. Which we don't."

"*You* don't."

"Neither of us do," she reiterated. Although, she wasn't quite sure that was true. The fact was, Kent had asked her out a couple of times in the past few years. She'd figured that he was bored and that he'd thought she was, too. She'd said no every time, and he hadn't seemed at all heartbroken.

"I think he might say something different, if I asked him," Jackson commented casually, but there was nothing casual about the look in his eyes.

"Why would you?"

"Because someone is stalking you, and stalkers are generally not strangers. If he has a thing for you, maybe he's not willing to accept that you don't return his feelings."

She laughed. She couldn't help it.

Kent? A stalker?

He had dozens of women begging for his time and attention. He certainly didn't need her.

"What's so funny?" Jackson asked, crossing his arms over his chest, his biceps bulging beneath the sleeves of his dark T-shirt.

Was it her fault if she noticed?

She glanced away, surprised and a little appalled by just how attracted she was to him.

"The idea that Kent would be desperate enough to stalk someone," she mumbled, hoping Jackson didn't notice how red her cheeks had gotten. "He's out with a different woman every weekend."

"That means just about nothing, Raina. Stalkers are mentally ill. They don't act like typical, healthy individuals."

He had a point. A good one.

"Kent is a doctor."

"Meaning?"

"He's not mentally ill."

"One thing does not preclude the other, Raina."

"You're right, but I'm too tired to discuss it, so I think I'll go tuck myself into bed for a couple of hours. You should probably do the same."

She took a step away, but he snagged her hand. "You forgot something."

"I did?" Her heart thundered, her mouth went dry and every thought in her head flitted away. Because he was there, so close she could see the fine lines at the corners of his eyes, the ridged edges of the scar on his temple.

"The door?" He gestured to it, turning the lock and then the bolt. "You did tell Kent you were going to keep things locked up tight."

"Right. I forgot."

"Forgetting isn't an option, Raina. Not until the police have a suspect in custody."

She nodded, because a hard lump had formed in her throat, and she couldn't speak past it.

Matt had never bothered with locks.

But, then, Matt had never worried that things would go wrong. He'd had the kind of trust in God that Raina had never quite been able to achieve—an all-encompassing belief that God was in control and that He would make things work out the way they should. Raina had been a Christian for so many years she didn't remember what it felt like to not be one, but compared to the deep, rich hues of Matt's faith, hers was a pencil drawing—all soft lines and gray tones.

Maybe she hadn't needed it to be more.

Until the accident, she'd been able to tackle just about any problem, handle just about any trouble. Matt had been a wonderful husband, but he'd spent a lot of time with his head bent over books and commentaries. He'd had more scripture memorized than any person Raina had ever known, but he could never seem to remember what day the car payment was due.

She'd loved him despite those things and probably because of them, but she'd been the one to hold down the fort, take care of the problems, put out the fires.

"Raina." Jackson touched her wrist, his fingers warm and just a little rough. "Are you okay?"

"Fine. Great," she lied, because she wasn't going to tell him that having him in her living room was reminding her of all the things she used to have, all the things she'd dreamed of when she'd been young and sure that she could make life work out just the way she wanted it to.

He eyed her for a moment and shook his head. "You don't look fine. As a matter of fact, you look like you've been rode hard and put up wet."

The comment surprised a laugh out of her. "I look like a tired horse?"

"You look like a beautiful woman who may need to be taken care of a little better," he responded, so sincerely her heart jerked. The hard, quick beat reminded her of shy first glances and giddy first words, of nerve-racking first dates and tender first kisses. It reminded her of dreams and hopes and yearnings.

"I take good care of myself, Jackson." She moved past him, walking to the fireplace and the oversize flower painting that Matt had hung there the first night they'd slept in the house.

"I'm sure you do," he said quietly. "Sometimes I open my mouth before I use my brain. Sorry if I offended you."

"Since when is calling a woman beautiful offensive?" She turned around, and he was still standing near the door, his arms relaxed, his expression open. She'd seen more than one side of Jackson. The tough protector, and now the easygoing boy next door. She wondered which one was really him. Wondered if maybe they both were.

He studied her for a moment, his gaze touching her hair, her cheeks, her lips.

"Never," he finally said. "But from the look on your face, I'd say I stuck my foot in something, and it wasn't anything pleasant."

That made her smile. "Not really. I'm just tired. Like I said, I need to tuck myself into bed and get some sleep. See you in a few hours, Jackson."

She walked out of the room even though she wanted to run. Walked to her bedroom even though she wanted to race there.

She closed the door quietly, her hands shaking. She didn't turn the lock. Jackson wouldn't open the door. He wouldn't even knock on it unless there was an emergency. She should have found that comforting, but she felt empty and old as she lay down on the bed.

Above her head, floorboards creaked as Jackson returned to his room. She tried not to think about him up there as she closed her eyes and willed herself to sleep.

# SEVEN

*"Mommy? Where are you? Mommy!"*

*Joseph called to her from the darkness, and Raina tried to run toward him, but thick trees surrounded her, the branches catching at her clothes. She couldn't move, couldn't free herself.*

*"I'm coming!" she tried to yell, but the words came out a whisper, the sound fading away before it even had time to form.*

*"Mommy!" he called again, and she jerked against the tree branches, realized they weren't branches at all.*

*A man held her, his arms viselike and hard, his grip unyielding. She struggled against his hold, twisting until she could see a featureless face and deep holes where eyes should be.*

Raina woke with a start, a scream dying on her lips.

She shoved the comforter from the bed and stood on shaky legs, her heart still thudding loudly in her ears. She thought about Joseph every day, but she hadn't had a nightmare about him in months. Now she'd woken to the sound of his voice twice in—she glanced at the clock— less than twenty-four hours.

She walked to the window, cracking it open and taking a few deep breaths of cold air.

"Just a nightmare. That's all it was," she murmured, willing her frantic heartbeat to quiet. Her words scared a couple of birds from the trees, and she watched them fly to the fence and land on one of the posts. They sat in the sunlight, enjoying the afternoon warmth. She wanted to shut the window, close the curtains and go back to bed, but Samuel was sick, and she had to get him in to see Kent. Otherwise, she might end up making a trip to the emergency room with him.

She changed quickly, sliding into jeans that were a little loose and a warm sweater that was more cozy than stylish. She wasn't out to impress anyone, but she ran a brush through her hair, applied a little blush and mascara. She didn't bother with foundation. It would take a boatload to cover the circles under her eyes or to give her complexion a healthy glow.

The house was still silent as she slipped into the hall, the quiet creak of floorboards as familiar as sunrise. She'd been hearing it for so many years, the sound barely registered. Samuel must have heard. His door opened, and he peered out, his face drawn, his eyes glassy with what looked like fear.

"Hello," Raina greeted him. "Did you sleep well?"

He nodded, his gaze jumping to a spot just beyond her shoulder and settling there. She knew what he was looking at. The family photo that hung on the wall. There'd been plenty of times when she'd thought about taking it down, but that had felt like too much of a betrayal, so she'd left it hanging.

"My family. I'm the only one left," she said.

"We are both left," he responded, his English thickly accented but very clear. He looked so young hovering in the doorway, a crutch tucked under one arm. She wanted to touch his forehead, see if he was still hot, but she was afraid of moving too quickly and too soon, of pushing herself into his life when he'd rather be left on his own. She was afraid of trying too hard and of failing, of proving to herself and to Samuel that she really had lost her ability to mother a young boy.

"We are together now," she pointed out. "So I guess neither of us are left anymore."

He nodded solemnly, but she wasn't sure that meant he agreed.

She ran a hand over her hair, feeling unsure of herself and hating it. "So how about we go have something to eat and then I'm going to bring you to the doctor."

"No," he replied.

"No to food or no to the doctor?"

"No doctor."

"I'm sorry, Samuel, but you are going to the doctor. You have an infection, and if we don't get it healed, you won't be able to be fitted for your new leg."

"No doctor," he repeated as if he really thought he was the one who'd be making the decision about it. She supposed that made sense. He'd told hospital workers that his mother and father had been killed when he was six. He'd been making decisions for himself for a long time, surviving what most children wouldn't have.

"Samuel—"

The doorbell rang, and Samuel grabbed her hand, his eyes wide with fear.

"What it is?" he asked, and she could hear the slight tremor in his voice, feel his muscles trembling. Something in her heart went soft, the feeling similar to the one she'd had when she'd seen Joseph for the first time, his newborn baby face red from his frantic cries.

"Just the doorbell," she reassured him, gently squeezing his hand. "Someone is here for a visit. I need to go see who it is."

"I will come, too," he said stoically, and she

wondered if he thought he would need to protect her from whoever stood on the other side of the door.

"It's okay. I'll be fine. You get ready for our doctor's visit."

"No doctor!" Samuel muttered under his breath, but he hopped back into his room and closed the door.

Gently.

Thank goodness.

The doorbell rang again, and she ran down the hall, peering through the peephole. Andrew stood on the front porch, uniform hat pulled low over his eyes, hands shoved in his coat pockets. He didn't look happy.

She opened the door, her stomach churning with nerves. "Andrew! What are you doing here?"

"Freezing," he replied drily. "Mind if I come in?"

"No. Of course not." She gestured for him to enter. "Is everything okay?"

"You want me to beat around the bush or just give it to you straight?"

She wanted him to tell her that nothing was wrong, that he was just checking in, making sure that she was okay. That wasn't going to happen, though. She could see it in his eyes—bad news and sorrow. "Give it to me straight."

"Butch is dead."

The words were so blunt and so unexpected she couldn't quite process them. "What?"

"Butch Hendricks. He's dead."

"I just saw him a few hours ago. He was fine." Even though he'd repeated it, she could barely comprehend that the man who'd been part of the community, who'd stood on Main and Third asking for handouts for as long as she could remember, was gone. "Are you sure it's him? Maybe—"

"Raina," Andrew interrupted. "Do you really think I'd be here telling you this if I wasn't sure?"

"I… No. What happened?" She dropped onto the couch, and he took a seat across from her.

"The medical examiner will determine that." He rested his elbows on his knees, his hands clasped together. He looked exhausted, his eyes deeply shadowed, his jaw scruffy with the beginning of a beard. He hadn't shaved, probably hadn't been home.

"You must have some idea, Andrew," she pressed. "Or you wouldn't be here."

"There was no sign of foul play, but I don't like the way this is shaping up."

"The way what is shaping up?" Jackson walked into the room, still dressed in the jeans and black T-shirt he'd been wearing the night before. Just like Andrew, he was sporting a day's worth of beard growth. It didn't make *him* look tired or worn. It made him look...masculine, rugged. Sexy.

"Miller," Andrew acknowledged with a slight nod in Jackson's direction. "We were discussing Butch Hendricks. Specifically, his death."

"What happened?" Jackson walked farther into the room, his movements lithe and powerful. Even without trying, he looked strong. Even when there was no danger, he looked like the kind of guy who could face down just about anything or anyone and come out on top.

"He died sometime early this morning. That's all I know."

"He was right as rain when he left the church. That was only six hours ago."

"A lot can happen in six hours, Miller. I think you know that. The medical examiner is working on cause of death. I'll let you know his findings once I have them."

"You don't think it was a coincidence and you don't think he died of natural causes, do you?" Jackson asked, dropping onto the sofa next to Raina.

"I'm not going to speculate."

"Sure you are. You're just not going to do it on the record."

"You want off the record?" Andrew scowled.

"I'll give it to you. He either died of an overdose or was murdered."

Murdered?

Raina tensed at the word, every muscle balled up so tight she thought she'd shatter if she tried to move.

"Relax," Jackson whispered, his breath ruffling the hair near her ear. "Everything is going to be fine." He smoothed a hand up her arm, his fingers kneading the muscles in her neck.

Andrew noticed.

Of course he did.

Raina should have cared, but she didn't.

"Were you the one who found Butch?" Jackson asked, his palm resting against the corded muscles in Raina's shoulders. She was wound up tight, her eyes shadowed, her face drawn. If she'd slept at all, it hadn't been much.

"No. Another officer found him while the evidence team was processing an abandoned blue Jeep that fit the description and photo you provided."

"Kent mentioned that you'd found the Jeep," Raina said quietly.

"I saw him drive past in that fancy sports car of his. Didn't realize he was on his way here."

"He wanted to check on Samuel," Raina said, and Andrew laughed.

"Right."

"He did," Raina protested, her hands fisting in her lap. In Jackson's opinion, she needed some of the chamomile tea Grandma Ruth was always drinking. According to Jackson's mother, it was great for calming nerves.

"Maybe, but he also came to see you. He's a good guy, Raina, and there's nothing wrong with spending some time with him."

It was Jackson's turn to tense up.

He didn't like the idea of Raina and Kent getting together. He didn't like it at all.

"Except that I don't want to spend time with him, so how about we get back to what you came here for."

"Right." Andrew sighed. "We pulled a couple of prints from the Jeep. We'll try to run them, but it was reported stolen from D.C. about a month ago. It could have been in any number of hands since then."

"D.C.?" Jackson's pulse jumped and he met Raina's eyes. "Isn't that where your friend's boyfriend lives?"

"Are you talking about Lucas Raymond?" Andrew asked, and Raina nodded.

"He's the only one I know who owns a blue Jeep."

"I hadn't thought of that, but you're right. He's been driving that thing for years." Andrew pulled a notebook from his pocket and jotted something in it.

"You're not actually going to question him? If he were going to do something like this, don't you think he'd use a different car?" Raina sounded horrified.

"Maybe. Maybe not. Criminals make mistakes all the time. This might have been his."

"Destiny will have your hide if you call him."

"Why would she?" Andrew shrugged. "They broke up two weeks ago."

"What?" Raina jumped up, and Jackson stood with her. "Why didn't she tell me?"

"You were getting ready for Samuel's arrival. She didn't want to add more to your burden."

"She's my best friend!"

"And she was trying to protect you." Andrew stood, tucked the notebook back into his pocket.

"I don't need protecting."

"Tell her, then. I'm going to the office. I want to make a few phone calls, see if Lucas was home last night. I've never really liked the guy, and I wouldn't put it past him to pull something like this in order to force himself back into Destiny's life."

"How would chasing me through the woods accomplish that?" Raina asked.

"He's a psychiatrist. Maybe he's hoping to be called in for help with the case."

"Sounds like a stretch," Jackson said, and Andrew shrugged.

"Stranger things have happened, Miller, and as far as I'm concerned everyone is a suspect until I can prove they aren't."

"Are you including me in that?" Jackson asked, following him to the front door, Raina just a few steps behind.

"According to my sources, you've been here since six this morning. Butch died sometime after that, and since you obviously weren't the one driving the Jeep that almost ran you down—" he stepped out onto the porch "—I think I can remove you from my list."

"Thanks," Jackson responded drily. "Glad to hear it."

"Now that we've gotten that cleared up, I've got to head out."

He jogged down the porch steps and got in his squad car. Jackson wanted to get in his SUV and follow. He had more questions to ask. About Butch's death, about Lucas Raymond, about the stuffed dog that had been left in the woods.

"You know what I need?" Raina asked so quietly he almost didn't hear her.

"What?" He looked into her eyes, saw the fear and anxiety there, wanted nothing more at that moment than to chase it away. "Name it, and I'll get it for you."

She cracked a smile, her eyes crinkling at the corner, a tiny dimple appearing at the corner of her mouth. "You're tempting me to ask for the moon."

"If I could, I'd wrap it in a bow and put your name on it."

"Don't be so charming, Jackson," she responded, the smile faltering but not quite disappearing. "It could get us both in trouble."

"I love trouble. Ask Stella. She'll tell you all about it."

She shook her head and sighed, hooking her arm through his and tugging him into the kitchen. "Then I guess it's a good thing for you that all I want is a cup of black coffee and three minutes with absolutely no drama."

"That," he said, taking her hand and kissing her knuckles, "can absolutely be arranged."

# EIGHT

Raina got her coffee.

She even got her three minutes without any drama.

Things went downhill from there.

It started with Samuel having a major meltdown about the doctor visit and ended with an endless battle with Jackson about whether or not she needed an escort.

"I don't need you to come with me," she said for the fiftieth time as she grabbed her coat from the closet. "I don't," she repeated.

"Okay," he responded, finally conceding the point.

"I'm glad you're finally seeing it my way," she responded, but she didn't feel glad, she felt anxious and antsy.

"Why wouldn't I?" he responded, helping her into her coat and pulling the collar up around her neck, his fingers sliding against the tender flesh behind her ear. "If you want to go off unprotected with a vulnerable young boy, that's your business, and it's on your head if something happens to him."

"You're playing dirty," she accused, but he had a point, and she knew it. Samuel was her responsibility, and she couldn't risk his life because she needed a little…breathing room.

"I'll play any way I have to to keep you and Samuel safe."

"Fine. You can come," she agreed, and she didn't feel nearly as irritated about it as she probably should have.

"I'm glad you're finally seeing things my way," he said with a grin. "I'm going to check in with Stella. You get Samuel. I'll meet you back here in five."

He bounded up the stairs, and she headed down the hall, not realizing she was smiling until she reached Samuel's door.

She shook her head, exasperated with herself.

If she wasn't careful, Jackson would charm his way deeper into her life than he already had.

She shouldn't want that to happen, but there was a tiny part of her heart that didn't think she'd mind much if it did.

She knocked gently on Samuel's door. "Ready to go, Samuel?" she called.

He didn't answer, and she turned the knob,

frowning when she realized it was locked. She knocked again, cold air tickling her bare toes.

Had he opened the window? "Samuel?"

Still no answer, but she could definitely feel cold air drifting under the door.

She ran back to the kitchen and out the door, rounding the corner of the house at breakneck speed, her breath catching as her worst fears were confirmed. The window was open, the room beyond empty.

"Samuel!" she shouted at the top of her lungs, pivoting to the left and right, trying to decide which direction she should go. She thought she saw a speck of color in the trees at the back edge of the property, and she raced toward it, screaming his name so loudly the sound tore from her throat.

She'd hung his coat in the closet the night before. He didn't have a hat, gloves. He didn't know the area, knew nothing about the climate. He could get lost in the woods, be stranded all night without any way to keep warm.

She raced into the trees, and it was like her nightmare, branches snagging her shirt and poking at her legs, her heart pounding frantically. She fought through the foliage, searching the trees for signs that Samuel had been there.

"Raina!" someone shouted, but she didn't have

time to stop. If she didn't catch up to Samuel now, he could be lost for good.

"Raina!" Jackson grabbed her arm, yanking her to a stop. "Where do you think you're going?"

"To find Samuel." She tried to jerk away, but he didn't release his hold. "He climbed out his window and—"

"He's in the house."

"No. He's not." She yanked harder, but his fingers were firm around her biceps, the grip tight without being painful.

"He is. He came out of the bathroom as I was heading down the hall."

"Are you sure? I could have sworn I saw him running through the trees."

"Positive." His hand slipped from her arm, burrowed under her coat and rested on her waist. She could feel its heat through her cotton shirt.

"I can't lose another child," she said, the words like shards of broken glass—hard and brittle.

"You won't," he responded, pulling her close, pressing her head against his chest. She could hear his heart beating beneath her ear, and she wanted to close her eyes, pretend she was in a place where she could believe forever existed, believe that love could last, believe that her heart would never be broken.

"I'm okay," she said, but she didn't move. Her

legs were too shaky, her head still filled with memories of the nightmare and with fears of what might have been if Samuel really *had* wandered away.

She took a deep breath, inhaled masculinity, soap and some indefinable scent that reminded her of safety and of home.

Her eyes burned with tears, and she forced herself to step away. "I'm sorry," she said.

"Why?"

"Because I just had a major freak-out over nothing."

"His window was open. You thought he'd run away. That's not nothing." He glanced around the copse of trees, his jaw tight, his shoulders tense.

"Is something wrong?" she asked, a niggle of fear crawling up her spine.

"Probably not."

"That's not the same as *definitely* not."

It wasn't, because Jackson wasn't sure that there *was* nothing wrong Something felt off. He could feel it in the air—a hint of danger. Even in the middle of the day, light streaming through heavy branches and boughs, the trees were thick enough for someone to hide.

He didn't like that.

Didn't like it at all.

"How about we head back to your place?" he said, avoiding Raina's comment.

"What's going on, Jackson?"

"I don't know, but I'd rather try to figure it out after I get you back inside."

"In other words, you're going to escort me to the house and then come back and look around."

"Exactly."

"What if I don't like your plan?"

"I don't think I asked your opinion."

She shook her head, short blond hair fluttering around her face. "That's not the way this is going to work."

"The way *what* is going to work?" he asked, hurrying her back toward the house. The sooner he got her there, the happier he'd be.

"This." She waved her hand around as if that answered the question. "You going off and risking your life, and me cowering in the house, waiting for you to return. That's not the kind of person I am."

"Good to know." He opened the door, lifted her off her feet and deposited her inside.

"Hey!" she protested, but he was already closing the door and texting Stella to make sure she kept everyone inside.

He searched for thirty minutes and came up empty. He should have been relieved, but he wasn't. Someone had been in the woods with them. He was almost sure of it. He walked across the yard, stood near the back door and stared out into the gnarled orchards.

"Come on," he muttered. "Show yourself."

"You talking to yourself, Jackson?" Stella yelled through the kitchen window.

Was he?

He didn't think so.

He thought someone was out there.

He just needed a little more time to find the guy.

She opened the door, dragged him into the house. "What's going on?" she demanded.

"I don't know."

"But you're planning to stick around for a while to figure it out, right?" she responded, tapping her fingers on the counter impatiently. "Which means I'm stuck on the outskirts of some Podunk little town."

"I'm escorting Raina and Samuel to the doctor. After that, I'll bring you back to D.C."

"Sure you will," she said with a sigh.

"What's that supposed to mean?"

"You don't know how to keep your nose out of things, that's what it means. You see a kid and a woman in trouble, and you think you've got to drop everything to help."

"You're just annoyed because I won't bring

you home now. If you really want to get back to the city immediately, you can call—"

"Don't say it!" she barked.

"—Chance." He said his brother's name just to irritate her, because that's the way they were together.

"You're a pain, you know that, Jackson?" Stella growled. "For your information, I have plans this evening, and if we don't get out of here, I'm going to miss them."

"What plans?"

"Plans that do not include babysitting a grown woman and a kid and that do not include getting a ride back home with your brother," she hissed.

"I'll try to get you back to D.C. before sundown."

"Which means I'm either going to be here for the foreseeable future or going to have to hitchhike home," she muttered, obviously annoyed.

"I think you need some coffee."

"I think I need a new job and new friends. Maybe even a new life."

"Really?"

"I don't know. Ever since I met your brother, I've been in one mess after another. A girl doesn't always want to be covered with dirt and sweat. Sometimes she wants to wear sequins and heels."

"Stella—"

"Forget it, Jack. I probably do just need some coffee." She grabbed a mug, filled it with coffee and took a sip. "It's not very hot, but it'll do." She marched from the kitchen with her head held high, but Jackson had a feeling the things she'd said weren't just the rantings of a caffeine-deprived person.

She was right, too, and that made him feel guiltier than he wanted. In the years since she'd been part of HEART, Stella had spent more time rescuing other people's families than she had building relationships of her own. That got tiring. He knew it as well as anyone.

It was one of the reasons why he'd finally conceded the point and allowed Chance to give him a couple of weeks off.

He loved his job, but he needed more.

He needed...

What?

That was the question he couldn't ever seem to answer. Not without taking a long hard look at what he'd built. He'd gone into hostage rescue work because of Charity. He continued because it fulfilled him.

But there were times when he wanted more than his empty apartment and the quiet evenings alone. There were long days of travel when he wondered what it would be like to have someone waiting for him at the airport when he returned home.

He frowned.

Maybe Stella wasn't the only one who needed a cup of coffee.

# NINE

Life was spinning out of control.

That was the conclusion Raina came to as she sat in the exam room waiting for Kent to appear. Samuel sat on the exam table, stoic and silent, his eyes flashing with unhappiness. He didn't want to be there. He'd made it abundantly clear when she'd tried to get him into his coat, hat and gloves.

Jackson had finally managed to manhandle him into the coat, but the gloves and hat were still lying on the floor at the house.

She rubbed the back of her neck, trying to think of something to say. It used to be she had no problem with conversations. As a minister's wife, she knew how to talk to young people, old people, people in their prime and people near the end of their lives. There'd never been awkward silences or moments where she struggled to think of the right thing.

Back then, she'd thought she had the answers to lots of life's toughest questions.

She didn't think she had any answers at all anymore.

"Are you sorry you came to America, Samuel?" she finally asked.

He met her eyes, let his gaze drift away again. "No."

"You seem unhappy."

"No," he repeated, and she thought she heard a slight tremor in his voice.

"Are you scared?" She sat next to him, put an arm around his stiff shoulders. It felt uncomfortable, but somehow right, too.

"Yes," he whispered, his body sagging against hers. He probably weighed fifty pounds soaking wet. She felt every bone, every muscle.

Someone knocked on the door, the soft tap nothing like Kent's usual brisk rap.

"Come in," she called.

"Hey." Jackson stepped into the room. "You guys have been in here for a while. I thought you might be hungry." He reached into his coat pocket and pulled out two wrapped muffins.

She knew they'd come from a little diner that rented space in the basement of the building. She met Destiny there for lunch every few weeks. That was the thing about her friend. No matter how busy Destiny's schedule was, she always made time for Raina. Apparently, she didn't think Raina would return the favor.

Maybe she didn't think Raina *could* return it. After all, she'd seen Raina at her worst. Seen her huddled under blankets, sobbing into the mattress, hugging piles of clothes that belonged to her husband and son.

"I need to call her," Raina said as she took the muffin Jackson offered.

"Who?"

"Destiny."

"The friend who broke up with her boyfriend and didn't tell you?" He unwrapped the second muffin and handed it to Samuel.

"That's the one."

"You want to ask her why she didn't tell you?"

"I know why she didn't tell me. She didn't want to overwhelm me."

"Then why bring it up to her?" he asked.

"Because I want her to know I'm here for her."

"She knows."

"You've never even met her."

"I don't have to." He snagged a piece of her muffin and popped it into his mouth. "I've met you."

"What does that have to do with anything?"

"It has everything to do with it. Look what you're doing right now. You're sitting in a doctor's office with a boy you barely know.

That's not what someone who isn't there for her friends does."

She shrugged. "Maybe not."

"Definitely not." He took another piece of the muffin.

"I thought this was for me," she protested, and Samuel broke off a piece of his and shoved it into her mouth.

She was so surprised, she laughed, pieces of muffin falling onto the exam table and the floor.

"What's going on in here?" Kent peered into the room, a deep frown line etched in his forehead.

"Sorry. I guess we're getting a little silly from fatigue." She used a paper towel to wipe of the crumbs and tossed the mess into the trash can.

"You know you're not supposed to have food in here," he snapped as he walked into the room.

"My fault, Kent," Jackson offered, leaning his shoulder against the wall. "They were both hungry, and I wasn't thinking about rules."

"Maybe you should next time. This is a medical clinic. Not a diner." He shook his head disapprovingly. "You should probably wash your face, Raina. It's a mess."

"Why be rude, Doc?" Jackson said, straightening to his full height and taking a step toward him.

"I'm not rude. I'm honest. Right, Raina?"

She didn't plan to agree, so she just shrugged. She knew her boss. He snapped when things didn't go the way he planned. Obviously having people eating in one of the exam rooms wasn't part of his plan.

Samuel looked up from his half-eaten muffin, cocking his head to the side and studying Raina.

"You are wrong. She is not a mess. She is very beautiful," he said solemnly, his eyes the deep black of a moonless sky. He reached out, his fingers almost brushing her cheek before his hand dropped away, and her heart shuddered with the deep need to offer him comfort, security. Love.

"Like Sari," he mumbled, blinking rapidly and shoving a piece of muffin into his mouth.

"Who is Sari?" Jackson asked before Raina could get the words past the lump in her throat.

"My sister."

He had a sister? Raina had been told he was alone in the world, that everyone in his family had died.

"Is she in the refugee camp?" she asked, wondering if there was any way she could find the girl and bring her to the United States. Samuel might adjust better if he had someone familiar with him.

"She is dead."

"I'm…sorry." It was such a lame thing to say. Something she'd heard so many times after the accident that hearing it come out of her own mouth made her feel physically sick.

"I am sorry, too." Samuel slid off the exam table, tucking the remnant of the muffin into his coat pocket. "I think the doctor is not a good doctor if he thinks you are a mess. Let us return home."

"Wait a minute, young man," Kent said, closing the door before Samuel could escape. "I didn't mean a mess in the literal sense. I just meant she had muffin crumbs on her face. They're still there, by the way," he intoned with a frown in Raina's direction.

"You're right, Doc," Jackson responded, closing in on Raina and brushing his hand across her cheeks and then her lips. Her pulse jumped, a million butterflies dancing in her stomach.

"Better?" he asked, shooting a half smile in Kent's direction.

"Much," Kent said drily. "So how about we do what we're all here for. Take a look at that leg. Hop back up here, young man." He patted the exam table.

Jackson expected Samuel to balk, but the kid seemed to have finally accepted the inevitable. He clamored back onto the table, settling in a heap of bone and fabric. Kent frowned and brushed a stray crumb from the table before unpinning the pant leg that covered Samuel's stump.

Jackson found the guy supremely annoying, his facetious manners grating. If he'd known what a bottom-dweller the doctor was, he'd have brought some milk with the muffins. Maybe a piece of fruit or two and a few dozen saltine crackers. Just to get under the guy's skin.

Chance wouldn't approve, but he wasn't there to give a lecture on it.

Jackson backed up against a wall and watched as Moreland rolled up the pant leg that covered Samuel's stump. There were two raw wounds there. Both looked infected.

Jackson winced as Moreland swabbed both with antiseptic.

Samuel didn't move a muscle. Not even a twitch.

Raina, on the other hand, had her hands fisted so tightly the knuckles were stark white.

"Relax," he whispered, lifting one of her hands and trying to rub some blood back into it.

Moreland shot a look in their direction and frowned. "Want to come take a look at this, Raina?" he asked.

"Sure." She hurried over.

"We've got two infection sites here," Moreland said, as if it weren't obvious to anyone with eyes in his head.

"I noticed," Raina responded.

She didn't seem any more impressed with Moreland than Jackson was.

"I doubt it ever healed properly after surgery. I'm going to give him an antibiotic shot and write you out a prescription. I want to see him Monday. If things don't look better, we may have to have him admitted to the hospital."

"No hospital," Samuel said, his chin wobbling, his eyes filling with tears that surprised Jackson.

"Don't worry, sport," he said. "It's not going to come to that."

"Says who?" Moreland scoffed. "You? Because from where I'm standing that leg is getting close to needing more surgery. The likelihood that he'll end up in the hospital is pretty high."

Jackson hadn't been all that keen on the doctor when they'd met earlier. Now he liked him even less. Scaring a child who was obviously becoming distraught didn't speak well of the guy's character. "You're forgetting something, Doc," he responded. "Samuel is a tough kid, and he doesn't want to have surgery or spend more time in the hospital. He's going to take really good care of the leg."

"He's a ten-year-old boy. He has no control over the situation," Moreland said, not bothering to look up from a chart he was writing in.

"He's a smart ten-year-old, and he and I are

going to make sure that leg heals up just fine. Aren't we, Samuel?"

Samuel nodded, but Moreland was still too busy writing to notice.

"You're leaving town today, aren't you, Jackson?" Moreland asked, completely ignoring the comment and offering Samuel no reassurance.

Which annoyed Jackson even more than he already was.

"Yes," Raina said.

"Maybe," Jackson responded at the same time.

Raina frowned and swiped a strand of hair from her cheek. "You have to get back to D.C.," she reminded him. "You have a job and a house and—"

"My vacation starts Monday."

"Your house—"

"A one-bedroom apartment. I don't have a dog, cat or plant that needs to be taken care of." And he wasn't in all that big of a hurry to get back to D.C. Lately, he'd been missing the slow pace of rural life. He'd almost booked a flight back home, but his parents had taken their yearly pilgrimage to Cambodia to ask for information on Charity, and there was no one at their little place in North Carolina. He could have visited Grandma Ruth, but she was on a Disney Cruise with twenty of her closest friends.

"Whatever your plans," Moreland interrupted,

"I don't think you can change the course of Samuel's treatment. I'll write out the scrip and send Molly in with the antibiotic injection. Give me five minutes, okay?" He smiled at Raina and stalked out of the room.

"I think I ticked him off," Jackson commented.

"That's not hard to do." Raina touched Samuel's shoulder. "You okay?"

"Yes."

"When the nurse comes in you're going to have to have a shot of medicine. Do you know what that means?" She looked into his eyes when she spoke, her voice gentle, her expression soft.

He imagined she'd been like that with her son, and he imagined that it must have nearly killed her when she'd had to make the decision to disconnect life support and let Joseph go. There'd been a photo in one of the local papers—Raina saying goodbye to her son. The article had been about a mother's heart and organ donation, but it hadn't been able to capture the pain she must have felt as she'd made the choice.

She must have sensed his gaze. She glanced his way, offering a tentative smile. "If you want to go back to the waiting room, you can."

"Is that what you want me to do?" he responded.

"I—" Her cell phone rang, and she frowned,

pulling it from her pocket. "It's Andrew. I'd better take it."

She pressed the phone to her ear.

"Hello?" she said, her body tensing. "Yes." Her gaze locked on Jackson, her face losing all color. "Okay. I'll be there. Yes. I'll let him know."

"What is it?" he asked as she shoved the phone back into her pocket.

"Butch didn't die of natural causes," she said, her gaze darting to Samuel. "He was murdered."

# TEN

Murder.

Raina rolled the word around in her head while she waited in Andrew's cubicle. He'd already made it clear that she wasn't a suspect. She wasn't so sure about Jackson. Despite what Andrew had said earlier, he'd insisted on questioning Jackson behind closed doors.

They'd disappeared a half hour ago and hadn't returned. The way things were looking, Jackson might just be the prime suspect.

He might be the *only* suspect.

Thank goodness Stella had offered to stay at the house with Samuel. The last thing he needed was to sit in a police station for half a day.

"This is a mess," she muttered.

"What's that, dear?" Gretchen Sampson looked up from her computer screen. A gray-haired grandmother of ten, she'd been working as a receptionist for the River Valley Police Department for more years than Raina had been alive. Everyone in town seemed to know her, and she seemed to know everyone in town. If there was trouble, she knew it, and if someone was in need, she spearheaded the effort to help.

After Matt's and Joseph's deaths, she'd been the first on Raina's doorstep, offering a casserole and a hug. "Nothing. I'm just…worried about my friend."

"That good-looking guy Andrew is questioning?" She glanced at the interview room, her gray curls so short and tight they barely moved. "You've got nothing to worry about."

"Andrew seems to think he might have been involved in Butch's murder."

"Nah. He's just being cautious."

"I hope you're right."

"I know I'm right. I probably shouldn't say, but I heard Andrew talking to Garrison Smith. That young guy who just joined the force? Blond hair and brown eyes? Looks young enough to be in grade school?"

Raina knew who she was talking about. Garrison had transplanted from Miami a few months before the accident. He'd been on the scene when they'd pulled Matt and Joseph from the car, and he'd been with Andrew when he'd broken the news to her. "I know him."

"He found Butch facedown in a ditch beside the road. Pretty close to where you guys had that incident this morning. There didn't appear to be any trauma to the body, so Garrison assumed that Butch had died of natural causes." She paused, apparently waiting for some kind of reaction from Raina. When she didn't get one, she continued, "He did due diligence. Took pictures of the scene. Including a footprint in the mud near the body. After the coroner realized Butch had been strangled—"

"He was strangled?" That wasn't something Andrew had mentioned.

"Yes, and whoever did it wanted to make sure he was well and truly dead. His larynx was crushed. Poor guy." Gretchen blinked rapidly, and Raina was sure she was fighting tears.

"I'm so sorry that happened to him, Gretchen. No one deserves that kind of death."

"You're right about that. Butch might have been a drunk, but he helped me around my house after my husband died. Painted my barn one year and fixed the fence when it was coming down. He never asked for anything but a hot meal." Gretchen sniffed and wiped at her eyes. "But I'm getting off the subject. That print Garrison took the picture of? It didn't belong to your young man."

"He's not—" *Mine,* she almost said, but stopped herself before she could voice the protest. "How do you know?"

"Easy. Your friend was wearing boots, right?"

"Yes."

"Garrison said the print came from a running shoe. Nike, maybe. They're looking into it."

"It might not belong to the murderer," she pointed out, and Gretchen shook her head.

"You're wrong there, dear." She leaned forward, snagged Raina's hand and pulled her a step closer. "Now, you didn't hear this from me, but there was another footprint found. It matched the other exactly."

"Where did they find the second print?" she asked, her stomach turning. She'd been hoping there was no connection between Butch's murder and the man who'd chased her through the woods. She had a feeling those hopes were in vain.

"Right near where they picked up that stuffed dog of your son's."

"We aren't sure it belonged to Joseph." She'd thought it was his, but until she got a closer look, she couldn't be sure.

"It did. Andrew found a tag on it. Had your son's name written right on it in blue Sharpie. Joey Lowery. Looked like the little guy had written it himself."

He had.

The day he'd brought it to kindergarten for show-and-tell, he'd scrawled his name in uneven letters on the small tag. Since he hadn't been able to fit Joseph, Raina had helped him spell Joey.

She could remember it as if it was yesterday. The way he'd scrunched up his nose and stuck the tip of his tongue between his lips. The way the marker had slipped and left a trail of blue across the kitchen table. She'd scrubbed and scrubbed to get the mark off.

How she wished she'd just left it alone. That tiny little line that her son had made.

She blinked back hot tears, her chest so tight she couldn't breathe.

"Are you okay, Raina? You look pale." Gretchen stood and grabbed her arm, her chocolate-brown eyes filled with concern. "Sit down. Take a couple of deep breaths."

"No. I just need some air. Tell Andrew I took a walk. I'll be back."

"I don't think that's a good idea. He really wants to talk to you when he finishes with your friend," Gretchen called, but Raina wasn't in the mood for listening. She ran down a short corridor, slowed her pace as she walked into the lobby. A couple of people were sitting in chairs there, the late-afternoon sun filtering in through oversize windows.

She shoved open the door, the fall wreath someone had hung slapping against the glass.

The air had the cool, crisp feel of winter, and

she pulled her coat closed, zipping it up against the breeze. Downtown River Valley bustled with activity this time of year, people coming from D.C. and Baltimore to shop for antiques or peruse the artisan shops that lined Main Street.

She headed away from the busy stores, turning onto Elm Street. Matt's parents had once owned a house there. They'd sold it five months after the accident and used the money to buy a place in Florida. As far as Raina knew, they still lived there. She sent them cards for every holiday and birthday, but they'd changed their phone number and hadn't bothered giving her the new one.

In their eyes, she'd been the reason their only son and grandchild had died. If she'd been the happy little homemaker she was supposed to be, she'd have been home when Matt decided to take Joseph for ice cream. She wasn't sure what difference that would have made, but her in-laws had made it very clear that she should have either saved their family or died with them.

Sometimes late at night, when the house was quiet and her thoughts were loud, she was sure they were right. That she'd been the reason for their deaths. That if she'd just been less selfish and more devoted, Matt and Joseph would still be alive.

Hot tears burned behind her eyes, but she didn't let them fall. She'd already cried an ocean of tears and it hadn't done her any good. Keeping busy, being active and crawling into bed so exhausted she fell asleep before her mind could wander into dangerous territory was way more effective than crying a million more.

She pulled out her cell phone, dialed Destiny's number.

Destiny picked up on the first ring, just the way she'd known she would.

"What in the world is going on, Raina?" she nearly screamed into the phone.

"What are you talking about?"

"Did you forget it's the Harvest dinner for the singles group at church tonight?"

"I told you I wouldn't be there. I can't leave—"

"Samuel alone. I know. You've said it about a million times. That's not what I'm talking about. I'm at the church, cooking for this shindig, and Doctor Moron—"

"He is not a moron."

"Then he's an imbecile."

"Destiny!"

"What?"

"Just because you don't like him—"

"Since when did I say I didn't like him?"

"Every time I mention his name."

"I have nothing against him. I have everything against the two of you getting together. He's not the kind of man you need in your life. You need one that—"

"I don't need one at all," she cut Destiny off before her friend could go on another one of her "you need a good man in your life" diatribes. "And apparently neither do you. Andrew told me you and Lucas broke up."

"We didn't break up. I did. He's too controlling."

"You never mentioned that before."

"Because he wasn't controlling until I decided I wanted to spend a weekend in River Valley instead of going to some stupid psychiatric convention in D.C.," she huffed.

"Was that the weekend you helped me clean out Samuel's room."

"It was. Best weekend of my life, because I realized what a loser Lucas was and freed myself up for Mr. Right."

"Destiny—"

"Don't tell me I made a mistake, Rain. I didn't. If Lucas was the right guy for me, he wouldn't have left a dozen messages threatening to end it all if I didn't get back together with him."

"Did he really do that?"

"Of course he did. Said it was a joke when I called the police and reported a possible suicidal psychiatrist, but I'm not buying it. The guy is sick in the head, and I'm better off without him. Now, can we please get back to Moron More-land? He has called me sixteen thousand times trying to find out if I know what's going on with you."

"Are you sure it was that many times? Kent is a busy guy," Raina teased as she crossed Trent and continued along Elm. The houses were farther apart on this section of road, the lots at least five acres each. In the distance, the sun hung low over mountains cloaked in gold and red.

"You're missing the point, Rain," Destiny responded, not a hint of amusement in her voice.

"What *is* the point, then?"

"That something must be going on or he wouldn't be calling. So what is it and why did it take you this long to call me?"

"I was at the police station. I didn't want to call from there."

"At the police station?" Destiny nearly shouted. "Will you please tell me what's going on?"

Raina explained briefly. When she finished, Destiny was silent. Surprising, because her friend was almost never without words.

"Are you still there?" Raina finally asked.

"Yeah. I'm just not sure what to say except…wow!"

"Yeah. Wow."

"What is Andrew doing to find the guy responsible?"

"He didn't tell you?"

"Tell me what?"

"He's contacting Lucas."

"Because he owns a blue Jeep? My brother has gone off the deep end." She sighed.

"Does he know that Lucas—"

"Threatened to kill himself? Of course he does. He's the first person I told, and he's the one who told me to call the D.C. police."

"Maybe that's why he suspects him."

"Could be. Andrew is a pretty smart guy. His theories are usually pretty spot-on. I'm just not sure Lucas would go to such lengths to get my attention. Are you at the station now?

"No." And Andrew wasn't going to be very happy about that.

Neither was Jackson.

She glanced back the way she'd come. The street was quiet, the sinking sun casting long shadows along the pavement.

"You're at home?"

"I'm taking a walk."

"Are you crazy? Someone is after you, and you're on a leisurely stroll."

"I guess I didn't think things through very carefully."

"Well, you should have. You're my best friend, the sister of my heart. Anything happens to you, and I don't know what I'd do."

"You'd go on." *Just like I have,* she almost said. She didn't.

"I need to call my brother and put a burner under his behind. Maybe that stuffed dog will be the clue he needs to find the guy responsible. Goodwill should know who bought it. I still have the donation receipt the clerk gave me the day I dropped everything off there. I thought I'd wait a while to give it to you." She didn't say that she'd been worried about Raina's mental health, but they both knew it was true.

The room had sat untouched for almost four years. Cleaning it out for Samuel's arrival had been one of the most difficult things Raina had ever done. "The police will probably want it. Do you mind if I stop by your place and pick it up tonight?"

"You know you can, sweetie. And don't be sad, okay?"

"I'm not sad." She stopped in front of a white picket fence, looked into a yard she knew almost as well as she knew her own. The grass wasn't nearly as lush as it had been when her in-laws had owned the property, and the wraparound front porch looked gray and dingy. There were no curtains in the windows. No furniture that she could see. Someone had hung a for-sale sign near the edge of the property. From the look of things, it had been there a while.

"Then what are you?"

"Terrified?"

"I don't blame you. This whole thing is creepy. Who would want to scare you like this?"

"I have no idea." She opened the gate and walked into the yard. The old swing still hung from the porch ceiling, and she went straight to it, sitting down in her familiar spot, the old chains creaking a protest.

"Aside from us, who knew about Joseph's stuffed dog?"

"Andrew. My family. Probably a few friends."

"And anyone who read the local newspaper after the accident. Remember the picture they ran? The one with you standing near the wreck holding Joseph's dog?"

"Actually, I've been trying really hard to forget it." She'd been distraught. Her face had been streaked with tears, her hair a tangled mess. For weeks afterward, she couldn't walk through a grocery store or stop at a gas station without someone stopping to offer condolences.

"Well, you can't forget it now. That photo opens up a whole list of suspects. I'd say almost everyone in town saw it."

"I'll mention it to Andrew."

"You'd better, and you'd also better be careful. Someone killed Butch, and that same person could come after you next."

"I'll be careful," she responded, pushing against the porch floor, letting the swing rock back and forth.

A Jeep passed the house, moving so slowly it caught Raina's attention. Old and dark blue, it had seen better days, one backlight smashed, a dent in the back bumper, the license plate so covered by grime she couldn't read it. It couldn't have been the one that had nearly run Jackson down, but her pulse leaped anyway, her throat going dry with fear.

"Raina? What's going on?" Destiny asked.

"Nothing. It's just—"

The Jeep pulled into a driveway a few houses up, disappearing for a heartbeat and then reappearing. Pulling back out onto the road and heading back in her direction. She stood, backing up so that she was closer to the house and more hidden by its shadows.

"What?" Destiny nearly shouted. "Raina… seriously, you're freaking me out."

*I'm freaking myself out,* she wanted to say, but the words stuck in her throat as the Jeep slowly passed. It pulled into another driveway, and her heart nearly jumped from her chest as it reappeared, crawled toward her.

"Call the police," she managed to whisper through her terror. "I'm at Matt's parents' old house on Elm Street and there's—"

The Jeep stopped in front of the house, and she could see a figure in the driver's seat.

"And what? Raina! What's going on?"

She would have answered, but the door to the Jeep opened and the driver got out. Black pants, black shoes, a black coat that hid his build. He was tall, that was all she knew for sure, and he was wearing a hood, a mask, gloves.

She reached for the front doorknob, her heart slamming against her ribs, her blood pulsing with fear.

"Have you missed me?" he asked, his voice the soft raspy warning of a snake waiting to strike.

She yanked at the door handle.

Locked!

She pivoted, rounding the side of the house, jumping from the back edge of the porch, footsteps pounding behind her.

Something snagged her coat, and she was yanked backward.

"You shouldn't ignore me," he hissed in her

ear, his forearm pressed around her throat. "You should never ignore me."

She struggled to breathe, to think, to free herself.

In the distance, sirens shrieked, but she could barely hear them over the pulse of blood in her ears.

She jabbed her elbow into soft flesh, slammed her foot on his instep.

He groaned, his grip loosening just enough for her to gulp air, just enough for her to scream.

He shoved her forward with so much force she nearly flew, her shoulder knocking into the old oak tree Joseph used to try to climb, her head smashing into bark Matt had once carved their names into.

She saw stars, and then she saw nothing at all.

# ELEVEN

Jackson pulled up behind Officer Wallace's police car and jumped out of the SUV, bypassing an old blue Jeep as he followed Wallace across the yard. Thank the Lord he'd insisted on driving his own vehicle to the police station. Otherwise, he'd have had to find another way of getting to Raina.

He didn't think Wallace would have been amused if he'd hot-wired a car.

"Go back to your vehicle," Wallace yelled, but Jackson had no intention of obeying orders.

He'd played along, answered a million questions about a crime he'd had nothing to do with. He was done playing. Raina was in trouble, and he wasn't counting on anyone but himself to get her out of it.

"I said—"

"Let's split up. You take the left. I'll take the right," Jackson cut him off.

"I don't like this, Miller. You get hurt, it's on

your head. You get Raina hurt, and I'll throw your butt in jail and let you rot there," Wallace muttered, but he headed to the left and eased around the corner of the house.

Jackson moved to the right. His Glock had been confiscated at the police station, but he'd faced worse situations without it. Not an ideal scenario, but he'd make it work.

A saggy wraparound porch butted up against faded wood siding, mature trees growing so close to the house that their branches touched the windows. He stepped out from their shadows, scanning the backyard, Officer Wallace in his periphery. Raina was somewhere nearby. She had to be. That she'd been kidnapped again, was being held against her will again, wasn't something he wanted to contemplate.

He stepped farther into the yard, spotted what looked like a pile of fabric near the trunk of an old tree. No. Not fabric. Jeans. A coat. White-blond hair.

"Raina!" he shouted, sprinting toward her.

She sat up slowly as he reached her side, her eyes glazed, blood dripping down her forehead. He pulled off his coat, pressing the sleeve against her forehead.

"Ouch!" She batted at his hand, but he held firm.

"You're bleeding."

"You're going to be bleeding, too, if you don't stop adding to my headache," she mumbled, some of the color returning to her face.

"Are you threatening me, Raina?" he asked, sliding his free arm around her waist, relief coursing through him.

"I might be," she muttered. "I get grumpy when I'm in pain."

"Good to know." He pulled his coat away from her forehead, eyed the shallow gash. "I don't think you're going to need stitches."

"Also good to know," she responded with a slight smile.

"You might have a scar, though."

"I'd rather have the kind that can be seen than the kind that can't be." Her eyes drifted closed, and his heart jerked with fear. He'd watched people die from wounds that seemed minor, and he wasn't going to let that happen to Raina.

"How is she?" Wallace crouched beside him, his jaw tight, his expression grim. "I've already called for an ambulance."

"I don't need an ambulance." Raina's head came up like a shot, all the color that had returned to her face gone.

"Yes, you do," Jackson told her, pressing the coat back to the wound on her head. "You're bleeding like a stuck pig."

"Head wounds always bleed a lot." She nudged

his hand aside and held the coat sleeve herself. "I'll go home, slap a Band-Aid on it and be good to go."

She tried to get to her feet, but he tugged her back. "Whatever you're thinking, it's not going to happen."

"I'm thinking that I'm going home, and I'm thinking it *is* going to happen," she insisted, but she didn't try to stand again.

"Did you see the man who attacked you, Raina?" Andrew changed the subject, his voice hard and just a little sharp.

"Not his face. He was wearing a ski mask."

"How about his eyes?"

She shook her head. "He grabbed me from behind, and I was too busy fighting to notice much." Her voice shook, and Andrew patted her shoulder.

"It's okay. We'll talk more after the doctor takes a look at your head."

"I already told you, I'm not going to the hospital."

"You don't have a choice, Raina. We've got a victim's advocate waiting there."

"Tell him to meet me at my place or at the police station."

"Sorry," he responded. "It's not going to happen that way."

"I'm not—"

Sirens blasted through the afternoon quiet, and Andrew glanced over his shoulder. "I'll let the EMTs know you're back here. Sit tight."

"I don't think so," Raina mumbled, easing away from Jackson's arm and struggling to her feet.

He followed her up, setting his hands on her waist when she swayed. "You're not thinking clearly."

"I hate hospitals, and I don't want to be in one," she replied, her voice breaking.

"You worked in one for a few years," he pointed out, gently brushing strands of hair from her forehead. The wound had already stopped bleeding, but the skin looked raw and swollen, the flesh bruised. She'd hit her head hard.

"That was before."

"Before your husband and son died?"

"Yes."

"Just because they died doesn't mean you will. You know that, right?"

"It has nothing to do with that, Jackson. Nothing at all."

"Then what does it have to do with?"

"You want to know the truth?"

"That would be a lot better than a lie."

She didn't even crack a smile. As a matter of fact, he wasn't sure she was really listening to his words or paying attention to her own. She seemed far away, her gaze fixed on some distant point. "I hate hospitals because they remind me of what a failure I am."

"A failure? What's that supposed to mean?"

"It means my son died right in front of me, and I couldn't do anything about it."

Her words speared straight into his heart.

He knew what it was like to live with guilt, to think there was something more that could have been done, some solution that could have been found that would have changed things for the better.

"Raina—"

"Don't, Jackson." A tear slid down her cheek, dripped onto the ground near their feet. "Nothing you say can change how I feel."

"I know." He tugged her into his arms, and she rested her cheek on his chest. "But nothing you feel can make what happened your fault, either."

She tensed, then relaxed against him, her arms sliding around his waist, her hands drifting to his back. Voices carried into the silence, the sounds of the ambulance crew mixing with Wallace's deep commands, but she didn't move, and Jackson didn't feel the need to make her. Standing there with her felt more like coming home than anything had in a very long time.

"Sir?" A young dark-haired woman appeared

at his elbow. "We're going to need to take a look at the patient."

He released Raina reluctantly, stepping back as two men moved in.

"Did she say anything else to you?" Wallace asked, his tone grim.

"Nothing that will help."

"You know that I should arrest you for interfering with an investigation, right?" the older man growled, his gaze on the ambulance crew and Raina.

"I didn't interfere."

"You didn't stay out, either."

He had a point, but Jackson wasn't going to apologize. He'd done what he'd felt he had to do, and he'd do it again in a heartbeat. "Just so you know, I'm not planning to stay out of it."

Wallace sighed. "Just do me a favor, will you? Be careful. I'm already dealing with one homicide. I don't want to deal with another."

"I'll be careful." He glanced past the officer, watching as the ambulance crew helped Raina onto a gurney. She didn't protest, just lay back and closed her eyes.

"Since you're here anyway, you want to head to the hospital with her? I'm going to look around, see what kind of evidence I can find."

"He left his Jeep. That should contain plenty," Jackson responded, his attention still on Raina.

"I'm calling in a state team for that. This is the second blue Jeep the guy has used. Maybe there's some message in that that I'm not seeing."

Surprised, Jackson met Wallace's eyes. "I'm glad to hear that you're calling for backup."

"I figured you would be." He lifted his hat, ran his hand over his hair. "But you're not going to be happy to hear this. I'm going to say it anyway, because Raina is like a kid sister to me. You hurt her, and I will have to hurt you, and I'm really not going to care if I go to jail for doing it. Got it?"

He got it, all right.

He had a kid sister.

He'd do anything to protect her, would hurt anyone who hurt her. "I get it, but you should probably get this—I don't walk away from people I care about. And I care about Raina. As long as she's in danger, I'll be around, and I'll be sticking my nose places you probably don't want me to."

Wallace shoved his hat back on, nodded curtly. "I hear you. Just don't break the law, and we'll be just fine."

The ambulance crew maneuvered the gurney past them, and Wallace nodded in their direction. "You'd better go. The victim advocate will be at the hospital, but I want someone Raina feels comfortable with to be there, too."

"You want to ride with us?" the dark-haired woman asked as they wheeled the gurney onto the ambulance.

"Sure." He climbed aboard, took a seat on the bench the EMT indicated.

The ambulance doors closed, and Raina opened her eyes, looked straight into his. "I really don't want to go to the hospital."

"I know."

She scowled, but there was no real ire in her eyes. Just sadness mixed with fear. "I think you've got the story wrong, Jackson, because this is not how it's supposed to work out," she grumbled.

"How what is supposed to work out?"

"The epic adventure novel, Jackson. Get with the program," she huffed.

"And exactly how is the epic adventure supposed to work?

"The hero breaks down the door to the prison and carries the heroine to some safe hiding place."

"We've been there, remember? Now we're at the place where the hero tells the heroine that everything is going to be just fine."

"Yeah? Then why aren't we in some cozy hideaway?" She reached out a hand, and he took it, held it gently as her eyes drifted shut again.

"Because you need to be seen by a doctor."

"Since you seem to have all the answers," she said so quietly he almost didn't hear, "what's the next part of the story?"

"I guess," he responded, "that depends on what kind of ending you want."

She nodded, but didn't open her eyes.

Didn't say another word as the ambulance engine roared to life and the driver sped toward the hospital.

# TWELVE

Obviously she was going to live.

That being the case, Raina wanted out of the hospital.

Not in five or ten minutes, either.

Right at that moment.

The problem was, a victim's advocate had greeted her at the hospital and collected her clothes. Everything from the skin out had been taken, put in a bag and carried away.

Which left her sitting on the exam table wearing a cotton hospital gown and a bandage. Since the bandage was on her head, it wasn't covering much.

She glanced at the clock. She'd called Destiny twenty minutes ago, and her friend had promised to bring clothes. She hadn't arrived yet.

Or maybe she had and the police weren't letting her into the room.

Whatever the case, Raina was getting just desperate enough to take matters into her own hands. She jumped off the exam table, wincing as pain shot through her head. No concussion. No skull fracture. Nothing but a nice little goose egg and some scraped skin. It hurt plenty, though.

She walked to the door, thought about opening it and just…leaving. The problem was, she didn't think she'd get far dressed in a hospital gown. Especially not when she'd been brought to River Valley General, a place where just about everyone knew her. Not one of them would be willing to let her leave without telling the police that she was going.

The sound of a child crying drifted through the closed door, and she wanted to cover her head with the blanket one of the nurses had brought for her, do everything in her power to drown out the noise.

Joseph had been crying when they'd brought him in.

Calling for her, and she'd run to him.

He hadn't known she was there. No matter how many times she'd called his name, touched his battered head and bloody cheek, he hadn't known.

Her throat closed, and she opened the door. Not caring what she was or wasn't wearing. Not caring about anything but getting out of that room, away from that sound.

"Hey!" Warm hands wrapped around her waist, pulling her up short. "Where do you think you're going?"

She looked up into Jackson's dark blue eyes, and all the tears that had been clogging her throat burst out.

"I need some air," she managed, the words nearly choking her.

He took off his coat, dropped it around her shoulders. "Then let's get some for you."

She was in his arms before she realized what he planned to do, out the door of the hospital before she could think to protest. The tears were still pouring down her face, and her body was shaking, and she was really afraid that she would never breathe again.

"Shh," Jackson murmured, his breath ruffling the hair near her temple. "It's okay."

No. It wasn't.

It hadn't been okay for a long time, and if she hadn't been crying so hard, she would have told him that.

"Hey! You!" someone called. "Where do you think you're going with her? Put her down! I'm calling the police!"

Raina knew the voice.

Destiny.

She'd finally arrived, and from the sound of things, she was raring for a fight.

Jackson set Raina on the ground, shifting so that he was standing slightly in front of her. His shoulders and back blocked her view, but she knew they were in an alcove at the back of the hospital. She'd spent a lot of time there during the three days that Joseph had been in a coma, sitting on a bench, trying desperately to pray.

"Raina!" Destiny called. "I'll distract him. You run."

"No! Destiny!" But, of course, her friend was already barreling into Jackson.

To his credit, he didn't lose his balance and he didn't shove her back. He grabbed her flailing arms, holding them down as he sidestepped the foot she'd aimed at his shins. "Cool it, lady. I'm a friend."

"Friend? I know every one of Raina's friends, and you aren't one of them." Destiny ground the words out as she tried to loosen his grip. "Raina! Come on. I'll hold him for the police. You run."

"He's a friend, Destiny. Just like he said." She stepped out from behind Jackson, her legs a little wobbly, her heart a little wobbly, too. She hated the alcove, the hospital, all the memories that were there.

"How come I've never met him?" Destiny backed off, her curly black hair bobbing with the movement. At five-foot-nothing and less than a hundred pounds, she wouldn't have stood a chance if Jackson really had been a kidnapper.

Raina loved her too much to say that. "I met him in Africa."

"Oh." Destiny's brow furrowed, her dark eyes flashing. "That explains nothing."

"He brought Samuel to my place last night."

"I thought you'd hired a woman to do that."

"I did, but Jackson came along."

"And you didn't bother calling to tell me some good-looking, hunky guy was—"

"Tell you what, ladies," Jackson cut in, his arm sliding around Raina's waist, his fingers warm through the thin cotton of the hospital gown. "How about we get Raina back to the exam room? I'll step out, and *then* you can have a long discussion about me."

"Good plan." Destiny strode toward the hospital door and lifted a bag that was lying on the ground there. "These are the clothes you asked for, Rain. I just grabbed some of my stuff rather than driving out to your place. I figured that would save time."

"Thanks." She took the bag, thought about moving away from Jackson, but it felt good to have him there. She didn't want to think too much about what that meant. Not when she was so close to the place where she'd said her last goodbye to Matt, the place where she'd listened to her son call for her.

She swallowed back her tears, keeping her head down as Jackson urged her back to the exam room. Like every other room on the corridor, it was small. It felt even smaller with Jackson and Destiny there.

"I'll help her with her clothes," Destiny said, taking charge the way she always did. "You go wait in the hall." She tried to nudge Jackson to the door, but he held his ground.

"Is that what you want, Raina?" he asked, and she was tempted to tell him that being in the hospital had scrambled her brains and made her think that the only thing she wanted was to be in his arms again.

A silly thought. One that she'd be stupid to keep thinking. "Yes," she said, her mouth dry, her heart pounding, because she really didn't want him to leave.

"Okay." He touched her cheek, smiled gently. "I'll be right outside if you need me."

*I need you,* her brain whispered, but she shoved the words down and managed not to speak them.

"Wow!" Destiny breathed as soon as the door closed. "That is one fine specimen of a man."

"I guess." She shrugged nonchalantly, but she was feeling anything but nonchalant.

"You guess? *You guess?* Open your eyes and take a good look when he walks back in here. He is just about the finest-looking man I've seen around here in years."

Raina shrugged again and retrieved black skinny jeans and a fluffy pink sweater from the bag. "What in the world?"

"I was worried. I grabbed the first things I saw and ran with them. Hopefully, the jeans won't be too short."

"Too short? I don't think I can even get one leg in them!"

"Give me a break, Rain. You're skinny as a rail. So just shut up and get the clothes on. I want to see your man again."

"He's not *my* man!"

"Then why was he carrying you out of the hospital?"

"Because…I was upset. I heard a little kid crying, and it brought back a lot of stuff that I wasn't ready to deal with."

"Oh, honey," Destiny said with a sigh. "I'm so sorry."

"Me, too." She pulled on the jeans, managed to button them and still breathe. The sweater was soft and just a little loose, and it was so much easier to think about that than to think about Matt and Joseph. "Okay. I'm set."

"You don't have any shoes," Destiny responded

with a sly smile. "I guess I'm going to have to ask that hunk of burning love to give you a lift."

"Don't you dare," she responded, but Destiny already had the door open.

"Hey, Jackson! Raina needs you!" she called.

"I don't—"

Jackson stepped into the room, his hair a little mussed, his jaw dark with a beard. His gaze skimmed Raina's face, dropped to the pink sweater, the tight black jeans, settled on her feet.

"Shoe problems?" he asked with a half smile.

"I forgot to bring her some. Not that it would have done any good if I'd remembered. The girl has feet the size of—"

"I have perfectly normal-size feet, Destiny," Raina cut her friend off, her cheeks hot, her heart beating just a little too fast.

"You're right," Jackson said, moving so close Raina could see the fine lines at the corners of his eyes, smell the subtle scent of soap that clung to his skin. "They do appear to be just about perfect."

"That doesn't solve the problem," Destiny huffed.

"It's not a problem. Not yet. Raina can't leave until Officer Wallace speaks with her. He just called to tell me he's in the lobby and he wants us to wait here."

"Officer Wallace?" Destiny snorted. "My brother is a control freak. I never listen to him."

"He's your brother?" Jackson asked, looking as surprised as most people did when they found out the connection.

"Half, but we don't count that as any less than the whole thing." She tapped her finger against her lips and smirked. "Now that I think about it, I wouldn't want to annoy him. You two wait here. I'll go make sure he knows the way up here."

"You don't have to do that." Raina grabbed her friend's hand, but Destiny just smiled and pulled away.

"Of course I do. Sit tight. I'll be back in ten," she said with a wink that Raina was sure Jackson noticed.

She stepped out into the hall, offering a jaunty wave as she walked away.

"Well," Jackson said, that one word stretched out into so many syllables Raina couldn't help smiling.

"What?" he asked, taking her arm and leading her to the exam table.

"Your Southern accent is showing."

"Isn't it always? If not, my poor Southern grandmother will roll over in her grave." He smiled, lifting her onto the table.

"You really need to stop doing that."

"What?" He sat beside her, leg pressed to leg, arm to arm, and she wanted to smile again, because the room didn't feel so much like a triage room when he was in it. It felt more like…home?

She frowned. "Picking me up. You'll hurt yourself."

"You're kidding, right?" He laughed.

"No. I'm not kidding."

"I've carted two-hundred-pound men through enemy territory. I don't think picking you up is going to cause me any irreparable harm."

"That doesn't mean you should make a habit of it," she grumbled, and he laughed again, his arm settling around her shoulders, his palm resting on her upper arm.

"What if I want to?" he asked, all his amusement gone.

"Why would you?" She brushed lint from her jeans, her gaze on the floor, the wall, the ceiling. Anything but him.

"Because I think you're the kind of woman who'll understand what I do and why I do it," he said quietly, his fingers tracing a line along the inside of her arm.

She shuddered, a longing so deep, so undeniable filling her so that her heart ached with it. "Jackson—"

She wasn't sure what she planned to say, didn't know if she really had anything she could say.

She'd never know, because Kent stuck his head in the open doorway, his gaze jumping from Raina to Jackson and back again. "Am I interrupting something?"

"No." Raina jumped off the table, her head throbbing with the movement. "What are you doing here?"

"I got a call that you'd been hurt, and I came to check on you."

"A call from whom?"

"One of the nurses. Are you okay?" He moved into the room as if he owned the place, washed his hands as if he planned to exam Raina. Jackson didn't know much about medicine, but he didn't think Kent was going to find anything more than the E.R. doctor had.

He stepped between Moreland and Raina, offering a smile that he didn't feel. "It's nice of you to come check on her, but she's already been examined."

"I'm sure she'd like my opinion." Moreland frowned, his gaze settling on Raina.

She looked tired, her skin pale against the bright pink of the sweater she was wearing. A blue bruise peeked out from under the bandage on her forehead, and dark bruises marred her neck. The guy hadn't just slammed her head into a tree—he'd choked her. Jackson's skin tightened, anger burning hot in his gut.

"Would you like his opinion, Raina?" he asked.

She bit her lip, obviously uncomfortable with the situation.

Why wouldn't she be?

The guy was her boss. If she said she didn't want his opinion, that could cause problems.

"Raina?" he prodded, and she shook her head.

"I think I've had enough of doctors for the day. I'm sorry, Kent. It's nothing to do with you. I just—"

"No need to explain," Moreland said, his voice sharp. "I get it. I'm going to check on a patient who was admitted last night. If you change your mind in the next hour or so, give me a call."

He stalked from the room, his back ramrod straight, his steps brisk.

Jackson met Raina's eyes. "Hopefully, he won't hold that against you."

"He won't. He's not that kind of guy."

"What kind of guy is he, then?"

"Very focused. He loves his job, and he wants to help people."

"And what kind of guy is he to you?" he asked, because Kent was giving off all the signs of a guy whose territory was being infringed on.

"I already told you, Jackson. He asked me out a few times. I wasn't interested."

"When did he ask you? Before or after you went on the mission trip together?"

"Before. Why?"

"Just curious." And just thinking that Kent Moreland was a little too interested in Raina's life, that he spent a little too much time hanging around a woman who said she wasn't interested in him.

Andrew had his sights set on Destiny's boyfriend. Jackson thought maybe he should turn his attention in another direction.

"What are you thinking?" Raina asked, shifting so that she was facing him. Her eyes were the oddest color. Not quite blue. Not quite purple. They hid nothing. Not her sorrow, her fear, her curiosity.

"He seems to be spending a lot of time chasing after a woman who said she's not interested."

She shook her head. "He has just about every unattached woman in town chasing after him. I doubt he's that concerned with the one who got away."

"And yet he showed up at your house early yesterday morning, came to the hospital this afternoon. He said a nurse called to tell him you were here. Why?"

"Because he's an on-call doctor here, Jackson. He probably spends as much time at the hospital as he does at the clinic."

"Is this where you met him?" he asked, not sure if it mattered, but suddenly needing all the information he could get. Something was off about the doctor, and he planned to find out what it was.

"Actually, yes. He moved here from Wisconsin after his wife died. That was six or seven years ago. He started working as an E.R. doctor and opened the clinic a few years later. I met him my first day of work. We mostly just passed each other in the hallway, but after Matt and Joseph died…" She shook her head.

"What?"

"I guess he knew what it was like to lose someone. When I quit my job here, he offered to hire me at the clinic."

"And you've been working there ever since?"

"Actually, no. After the accident, I just wanted to hide away in my house with all my memories." She smiled, her eyes so sad Jackson touched her cheek, tucked a strand of hair behind her ear.

"You don't have to talk about this if you don't want to."

"I don't mind, and there's not much else to tell. One day, Destiny walked into the house and opened all the curtains and shades. She told me to take a shower and get ready, because she was bringing me to her church for a potluck. I was too tired to argue, so I went along with her. Kent attends the same church. He saw me, asked if I was ready to return to work."

"And were you?"

"I didn't think I was, but Destiny nagged me for a month, and I finally accepted the job."

"And went on a mission to Africa with Kent a few months later?"

"That was part of the church outreach program. I was sick of feeling sorry for myself and thought it would be a great opportunity to do something for others. It turned into more of a nightmare."

"You made it through, though, and you've brought Samuel here."

"Yes." She frowned. "I hope it works out. The visa is only for a year. I'm hoping someone from church will step forward and offer to adopt him. So far, people seem a little…worried."

"Because of his background?" he asked, glad that she'd thought beyond the year. Samuel deserved permanence and stability. Not just a year of wonderful living.

"Yes."

"Maybe once they meet him, they'll change their minds."

"I hope so. There's nothing for him in Africa but hardship, and he deserves a lot more than that."

"You could do it," he suggested, knowing he was stepping into something that he probably shouldn't and not really caring.

"No, I couldn't," she said simply.

He wanted to ask why not, but she'd closed up tight, her expression blank.

Whatever she was feeling, whatever she thought about offering Samuel a home, he wasn't going to get it out of her.

*Yet.*

Eventually, he would. When the time was right. When she wasn't so exhausted and broken.

Voices drifted from the hallway, and Jackson turned to face the doorway, expecting Andrew Wallace to appear.

Instead, a tall, dark-haired guy with an attitude peered in. The slightly shorter redheaded guy who stood behind him looked a little too amused for Jackson's liking.

A bad day had just gotten a lot worse.

"What are you doing here?" he asked, stepping back so his brother could enter the room. Daniel Boone Anderson sauntered in behind him, an annoying smirk still planted on his too-pretty face.

"Well, it's like this," Chance responded, his gaze settling on Raina. "Boone got a call from Stella. She said you were being questioned by the police. We left D.C. three hours ago and drove straight here."

"Because?" he asked, knowing it would annoy Chance and amuse Boone.

"HEART has a reputation to uphold, Jackson. You can't be dragged into the police department in every town you visit."

"And yet, he has been," Boone cut in, his grin spreading into a full-out smile. "How you doin', man?" he said, crossing the room and giving Jackson a smack on the back.

"I'd be better if you'd talked my brother out of coming."

"Hey, I just got back from Turkey. Been traveling three days. I can't be blamed for not thinking straight."

"Can we get back to the point," Chance interrupted. "How much damage has been done? Are you going to be arrested?"

"The officer in charge of the murder investigation will be here in a minute. Why don't you ask him?"

"Murder? Are you kidding me?" Chance looked as if he was about to blow a gasket, and Jackson decided to have pity on him.

"Don't worry, bro. I've already been cleared."

"Thank the good Lord for that."

Chance had barely gotten the words out when Wallace waltzed in as if he owned the place. Four grown men in a small triage area was about three too many.

Jackson would have volunteered to step out into the hall, but he wasn't going to leave Raina.

"Looks like you're having quite a party in here, Raina," Wallace said drily.

"I—"

Her response was cut off by a screech so loud it drilled its way straight into Jackson's skull.

"Fire alarm!" Boone shouted over the din. He glanced into the hall. "Smoke to the east. Let's move!"

No need for a plan. No need to discuss things. This was what the team did best, get people out of tough situations.

Jackson grabbed Raina, dumping her over his shoulder like a sack of potatoes as Chance ran into the hall. He followed, racing through acrid air and hazy smoke, heading west along the corridor, Chance a few yards in front, scooping up a little boy and clapping an arm around the kid's mother. Boone had taken up the rear. Jackson didn't have to look to know he was there. He could feel him like the air, the smoke, Raina's hands on his back.

He sprinted into the parking lot, set Raina down next to his brother.

"Keep an eye on her," he barked, and then he ran back inside.

# THIRTEEN

The sun had set hours ago, the waning moon creeping above the trees and settling there. Raina had been watching its slow march across the sky, counting as the minutes ticked by on the grandfather clock that sat in a dark corner of the room. She'd tucked Samuel into bed an hour ago, kissed his cheek because it seemed as though he needed someone to do it. To her surprise, a tear had slipped down his face, dropping onto his dark blue pillowcase. When she'd tried to wipe it away, he'd turned onto his side and covered his head with the blanket.

She'd wanted so badly to pull it back and tell him everything was going to be okay. She just hadn't known how to say it. Not to a child who'd lost everything, who'd been taken from everything he'd known and dumped in a new country with nothing but an old backpack and a few tired pieces of clothes.

She'd put her hand on his shoulder and left it

there, listening to his quiet sobs until he finally fell asleep.

Now she was at loose ends, waiting, wondering, worrying.

"Staring out the window isn't going to make any of them come back sooner," Stella commented. She'd stretched out on the couch, the quilt Matt's grandmother had made as a wedding present draped over her knees. A book in one hand, a bowl of popcorn in her lap, she looked completely relaxed and unconcerned.

"According to the news, three people were injured in the fire."

"Injured running out of the building. Not in the fire. There's a big difference."

"Either way, it could have been one of the men."

"Nah. I would have heard something if it had been." She stuffed a handful of popcorn into her mouth, held the bowl out. "Want some?"

"No. Thanks."

"Starving yourself isn't going to help, but suit yourself." Stella went back to her book, and Raina went back to the window. Across the street, Larry's lights were on, one glowing in the lower level of the house. Two in the upper level. That wasn't like Larry. He was a stickler for keeping lights off, eating at home rather than out and saving money any way possible.

He might not have been the most neighborly guy, but he was more than happy to share his opinions about things. Before Matt's death, he'd come over a couple of times to warn about the folly of leaving an outside light burning in the middle of the night.

"I should probably go check on him," she said. Not that Larry would appreciate it, but she needed something to do, and she really did want to make sure he was okay.

"Jackson doesn't need checking on. He knows how to take care of himself," Stella responded without looking up from her book.

"I was talking about my neighbor. He's been having some memory lapses lately."

"That's too bad, but you're not leaving the house."

"Says who?"

"Me."

"It's been a long time since anyone has tried to keep me from going out at night."

"You're misunderstanding, Raina," Stella said, finally looking up from her book. "I'm not *trying* to keep you from going outside. I *am* keeping you from it."

*You and what army?* nearly slipped out of Raina's mouth, but she didn't want a fight. Even if she did, she had a feeling Stella could take her down easily. "Fine. How about you go over and check on him?"

"I'm not supposed to leave you here alone."

"Says who?"

"Says Jackson."

"When did you speak to him?"

"I didn't. He texted me while you were tucking the kid in. Said they should be back in a couple of hours."

"Why didn't you tell me?"

"You didn't ask."

"Are you always this irritating?" Raina finally snapped, frustrated with Stella and with herself because she'd been pacing around worrying about someone who apparently didn't need it.

"Yes," Stella responded. "As a matter of fact, I am."

Raina bit her lip and kept her thoughts to herself, grabbing the phone and dialing Larry's number.

He didn't answer. Not surprising. He never answered the phone after eight at night or before nine in the morning. That was another one of the things that he'd made sure Raina and Matt knew.

She slammed the phone back into the receiver, and Stella scowled. "If I promise to go over there with you when the guys get back, will you relax?"

"That depends on whether you're any good at

keeping promises," she responded, pacing back to the window and staring out at the dark yard, the trees, the house across the street.

"I helped get your butt out of Africa, just like I promised your folks I would. I got Samuel to you safely, just like I promised you that I would. So, from where I'm sitting, I'd say I'm pretty good at keeping promises. Now, how about you sit down and be still so I can finish my book. If I can't be on a hot date tonight, I might as well read about someone who is." She stuck her nose back in the book, and Raina forced herself to perch on the edge of the couch and do absolutely nothing. No fidgeting, no toe tapping, no getting up to wash out the coffeepot or sweep the kitchen floor.

It had been a long time since she'd done that. As a matter of fact, she'd been going full tilt since Destiny forced her to get out of the house and get on with her life. She'd accepted a job at the clinic, gone on mission to Africa, spent hundreds of hours working to bring Samuel to the United States. She'd attended church, volunteered at local soup kitchens, created things to fill her time so that she wouldn't have to do exactly what she *was* doing—sitting in the silence and listening to her own thoughts.

Maybe she should have, though.

Maybe somewhere in the hollowness of her

grief, somewhere in the quiet loneliness of her new life, she'd find what she needed to move on and to heal.

Or maybe she'd just find a hundred reasons to crumble into a heap on the floor and cry until there weren't any tears left. That's what she'd been afraid of. That and the silence, because in it, she'd probably hear God gently nudging her soul, telling her that she couldn't waste her life because Matt and Joseph had lost theirs. She'd probably feel Him urging her back to the little church on the bluff, and the elderly congregation that hadn't been any more ready to let her go than she'd been ready to let go of her family.

Car lights splashed on the road, and Raina jumped up, watching as Jackson's SUV pulled into the driveway. A pickup truck and police cruiser were right behind it.

She opened the door, ran onto the front porch, waiting while the men got out of their vehicles. They all looked grim and tired. Even the redhead with the boy-next-door face and easy smile looked somber and serious.

Something was wrong. More wrong than a fire in a trash can at the hospital.

"What's going on?" she asked as Jackson jogged up the porch steps.

"Let's talk about it inside." He had a streak of soot on his cheek, and his eyes were shadowed with fatigue, but he still looked ready to do what was necessary to defend the people he cared about.

He also looked cold, his arms bare, his T-shirt no match for the chilly night air. She touched his arm, frowning at the icy feel of his skin.

"You're cold. I'll make some coffee for everyone," she said, leading the way back into the house and heading for the kitchen.

Jackson grabbed her hand, his fingers twining through hers. "We nearly drowned ourselves in coffee at the hospital."

"I could make—"

"Raina," he interrupted, his thumb skimming across her wrist, heat sliding up her arm and straight into the cold empty place in her heart. The place she hadn't ever wanted filled again. The place she'd locked up tight and ignored for so long she'd nearly forgotten it was there. "Just be still, okay?"

"You're the second person who's said that to me today," she responded, easing her hand from his and walking to the fireplace. There was wood in the firebox, kindling in the newspaper box beside it. She hadn't lit a fire in years, but a book of matches remained in the small box on the mantel, a lone match clinging to the cardboard. She set up the starter, lit the match, her hand shaking so much it went out before it ever got close to the kindling. She'd have to get another book from the kitchen, but first she was going to have to hear what the men had to say.

She turned back to the group, bracing herself as Andrew stepped inside and closed the door. She'd known him for enough years to read the frustration on his face, the fear, the worry.

Stella hadn't budged from her spot on the couch, but she looked up as the door closed, her gaze skirting past the man who stood beside Andrew. Raina hadn't been introduced, but Chance Miller had made his relationship to Jackson obvious. An inch taller than Jackson with pitch-black hair and bright blue eyes, he had the kind of face that could have been on magazine covers or on a Most Wanted poster for the FBI.

"It's about time," Stella muttered, dropping her book onto the coffee table and stretching. "Since everyone is present and accounted for, I'm going to get some sleep. Hopefully, when I wake up in the morning, I'll discover that being stranded on the outskirts of Mayberry is nothing but a bad dream."

"You promised you'd walk me over to Larry's," Raina reminded her.

"Right. Well, we can't do it now. Knock on my door when the men are done with you, but by that time, I have a feeling it will be too late to bother." She sauntered from the room as if she didn't have a care in the world, but her shoulders were tense and tight, her movements stiff.

Once she was gone, it was just Raina and four men who were all staring at her as if she was a bug under a microscope. She met Andrew's eyes, bracing herself for whatever it was he had to say. "What's going on?"

"I don't know how to tell you this, Raina," Andrew said, taking off his uniform hat and smoothing his hair. He tapped the hat on his thigh, exhausted, worried, tense. She wanted to tell him to relax, wanted to say that no matter what, everything would be okay. The words caught in her throat, though, fear keeping them trapped there.

"How about you just tell me?" she finally managed to say.

"You've heard that someone started a fire in a trash can at the hospital?"

"Yes."

"After the fire department put it out, they found some things."

"What things?"

He hesitated, then pulled a plastic bag from his pocket, set it down on the coffee table. "Take a look at these. Tell me if they're familiar."

She moved closer, her legs leaden, her heart racing.

A photograph nearly filled the gallon-size bag.

Face up, its edges charred, dark smudges coating the glossy finish, it was a wedding photo. Not just any photo, either. The one Destiny had snapped minutes after Raina and Matt had said their vows. Unposed, they'd been captured smiling into each other's eyes, his hand on her cheek, her hand on his waist.

"I will love you for eternity," he'd whispered just before they'd kissed for the first time as husband and wife.

She shoved the memory away, leaned to take a closer look at the photo. Aside from the charring and the smudges, it looked…off, and she couldn't figure out why.

"Can I touch it?" she asked, her voice thick.

"If you don't take it out of the bag."

She nodded, lifting the plastic bag from the table, realizing another photo was inside. She turned the bag over, her heart nearly stopping when she saw the picture. It had been taken by a photographer friend on Joseph's first birthday. The friend had insisted on doing an outside shoot, despite the fact that it was the middle of February. They'd bundled up and gone to the church, spread a blanket out in the yard, the cold watery sunlight dusting their hair and skin with gold. Joseph had taken his first steps that day, and it had been captured in the photo—a laughing little boy, his arms outstretched, four-toothed grin on his chubby face.

Only there was no face in the photo.

Not on the chubby little boy or on the man who stood in the background, both hands stretched out as he urged the toddler on. Both had been scratched out. Only Raina's face remained untouched.

She turned the bag over again, trying to see Matt's face through the layer of soot.

Gone. Just like in the birthday photo.

She dropped the plastic bag onto the table, stepping back so quickly, she bumped into someone. Warm hands clasped her upper arms, and Jackson's breath ruffled her hair. "You okay?" he asked softly.

She nodded, but she wasn't sure she was.

Andrew cleared his throat. Seeing the photos had to be hard on him, too. He and Matt had been good friends. They'd gone fishing together every summer, took care of the churchyard together. They'd met for breakfast the first Monday of the month for years. Raina wasn't the only one who had been left with holes in her life when Matt died. "These are obviously yours, Raina," he said. "What I need to know is whether someone made a copy of existing photos or took ones you had."

"I…" She glanced at the plastic bag, but didn't

want to touch it again. She could almost feel the vileness of the person who'd scratched the faces out. "Don't know. These are photos Matt kept on his desk at the church office. After he died, the office was cleaned out and his stuff was brought here. It's in boxes upstairs."

"You don't know if the photos were in the boxes?"

"I never looked. I can now, if you want."

"That's probably a good idea. I'm going to make a couple of calls. I'll be out on the porch if you find something."

"Okay." She didn't wait for him to go, just turned on her heels and ran from the room. She wanted to run outside, race through the trees the way she had in her dreams and in her waking nightmare. Maybe if she did, she'd somehow find a way to go back in time and return to the church while Matt's things were still in his office, those pictures sitting on his desk beckoning him to return home.

# FOURTEEN

"I guess you're going to want to take care of that," Boone said to Jackson, settling onto the couch and picking up the book Stella had abandoned there.

"Not before he explains how he got himself into this mess," Chance growled, dropping onto a chair. He had soot on both cheeks, and his white button-down shirt was probably permanently stained.

Jackson decided not to point it out to him. "Since it was Stella's idea to drive Samuel here from Atlanta and since it was her decision to pick me up in D.C. and bring me along for the ride, I'd say she's the one you're going to want to talk to about that."

"She went to bed. That leaves you." Chance tried to stare him down, the bright blue eyes that he'd inherited from their mother's side of the family nearly glowing with irritation. Charity had had eyes just like that. Only her hair had been deep auburn, her lashes golden rather than pitch-black. Thinking about their sister stole some of Jackson's frustration. Family was family, and it mattered more than minor irritations.

Or major ones.

The floorboards above their heads groaned, and he knew Raina was up there, digging through boxes that were covered with dust, looking for photos that she'd kept hidden away for years.

Boone was right. He *did* want to take care of it. "I'll explain the mess after I make sure that Raina is okay."

"Need any help?" Boone asked, grabbing a bowl of popcorn that had been left on the coffee table and shoving a handful into his mouth.

"No. Thanks."

He walked out of the room, half expecting Chance to follow him.

For once, his brother left well enough alone.

Maybe he was tired, or maybe he understood that what Jackson was doing had nothing to do with the case and everything to do with Raina.

He walked up the narrow stairs. There were only two rooms. The door to the one Stella was using was closed. Knowing her, it was also locked. The door to his room was wide open, light spilling out into the hallway.

Raina was sitting in front of the closet, an

open box in front of her, a picture in her hands. She didn't look up as he entered the room, didn't acknowledge him as he sat down beside her.

"It's hard, isn't it?" he said, taking the framed photo she was holding and looking at the little boy who smiled out from it. "I remember when I had to go to Charity's classroom and clean it out. She was a teacher, and she had photos on her desk and a few emergency candy bars in her drawer. She loved chocolate."

"Matt loved his family and he loved God." She lifted a well-worn Bible from the box and wiped dust from its cover. "Nothing else really mattered to him."

"And your son?" Jackson said, looking at the photo again. Joseph couldn't have been more than two when it was taken, his cheeks still chubby with baby fat. "What did he love?"

"Me." She offered a watery smile. "Matt. Everyone at church. He especially loved the older ladies who sat in the front pew. They always had butterscotch candy or gum for him in their purses."

She lifted a gold-wrapped butterscotch candy out of the box, tossed it back in. "I don't think I can do this."

"You don't have to," he said, wrapping an arm around her waist. "*We* will."

"It's been a long time since I've been part of a *we,*" she murmured. "I'm not sure I remember how it works."

He chuckled, pulling the box closer. "It's probably like riding a bike. Once you learn, you never forget how."

He lifted a handful of books from the box, checked through them to be sure no photos were stuck between the pages. "Your husband liked philosophy," he commented as he set the books to the side and lifted a few more.

"He liked studying. There are probably books on everything in there." She reached into one of the other boxes, pulling out a pile of framed pictures. "This is what we want to look through."

She handed him half the stack, and he pretended not to notice that her hands were shaking. He doubted she'd want it pointed out, and it wouldn't change anything.

He looked through one picture after another, family shots and portraits, a few of church activities. He tried not to look too closely at Joseph or to study the pictures of Raina for too long. They'd had a happy life, a good life, and it had been snatched away from them. Looking at snapshots of their life felt voyeuristic.

By the time they finished with the third box, Raina's hands were steadier, her gaze a little less haunted.

"I guess they're not here," she said, setting a watercolor of a butterfly on top of a pile of photos.

"It doesn't look like it." He stood, pulled her to her feet. "Do you know who packed the boxes?"

"Destiny and some people I worked with. I think Andrew was there. Maybe Lucas."

"Can you make a list of their names?"

"I have no idea who they were. Destiny brought the boxes to me and told me she'd had help," she responded, her hand still in his, her skin silky and soft and feminine enough to remind him of how much he missed having a woman in his life. "Andrew and Lucas were the only people she mentioned by name."

"Do you think she might remember who they were?"

"Destiny has a good memory, but it's been years." Her gaze dropped to the piles of things. "Funny how time passes and you don't even realize that it has." She sighed and tugged her hand from his. "I need to clean this mess up."

"I can take care of it."

"It's okay." She leaned over and grabbed a few of the books, dumping them into one of the boxes.

"Raina, it can wait."

He was right. It probably could wait, but Raina couldn't stomach the thought of leaving all of

Matt's things strewn across the scuffed floor. She picked up a few more books and tossed them on top of the first batch. She knew Jackson was watching, and she didn't care, because all she wanted was to put the boxes back in the closet, close the door and forget about them again.

"Cleaning up isn't going to make your problems go away. You know that, right?"

"I'm not trying to make anything go away."

"Except the past, and that's not possible," he replied.

She met his eyes, saw compassion written clearly on his face. He knew what she felt. He'd loved his sister, lost her, had to live with that every day.

"How do you do it?" she whispered, because she wanted to know. Needed to know.

"Do what?"

"Live every day knowing that your sister isn't around?"

"By living every day hoping and praying that I can keep other people from living the same way. By telling myself every single morning that God means for something good to come out of what happened and that the best thing I can do to honor my sister, the *only* thing I can do, is be a part of that. Come on. We need to go tell Andrew what we found." His hand settled on her waist, his thumb resting on a sliver of exposed skin between her jeans and her sweater.

It felt good.

So good Raina could have turned in his arms, let her hands settle on his waist, her head drop to his chest. Let herself enjoy, just for a minute, the feeling of not being alone.

Jackson's eyes darkened, his gaze dropping to her lips, his thumb sliding across that tiny bit of skin. Her breath caught, and she wanted to lean in and taste his lips almost as much as she wanted to turn and run.

"You better go down the steps first. The stairway is narrow," he muttered, his hand dropping away.

She nodded, her throat too tight to speak.

She had loved Matt with her whole heart, but with him, she had never felt the quicksilver heat that raced through her when she looked into Jackson's eyes.

She shivered, hurrying downstairs and stopping short when she reached the kitchen. All three men were there. Andrew, Chance and the redhead Jackson had called Boone.

He smiled, held up a package of cookies that she'd left on the counter. "I hope you don't mind that I snagged a couple of these. I'm starving."

"I can make you something."

"No," Jackson said as he stepped into the

room behind her, his arm brushing hers as he walked past. Her skin tightened, her body humming with an awareness she wasn't comfortable feeling. She'd closed herself off after the accident, locked herself in tight, because she hadn't wanted to risk her heart, hadn't wanted to ever again feel her soul shatter, her world shift, everything she'd understood be turned upside down.

"Boone is a food addict," Jackson continued. "If you start feeding him, you'll be feeding him from now until the cows come home."

"I resent that accusation, Jack. I might like to eat, but I can stop anytime I want to. The thing is, I don't want to." Boone pulled a cookie from the package and popped it into his mouth.

"I hate to interrupt the fun and games, folks," Andrew said. "But I think we have more important things to discuss than anyone's eating habits. Did you find the photos, Raina?"

"No." She opened the freezer and took out a plastic container of chicken noodle soup. It was so much easier to do that than to think about what those missing photos meant, to speculate on who took them and why.

"I helped Destiny pack the boxes, but most of the people there were your coworkers. Lucas was there. I remember that."

"I can ask Destiny who the other people were." She opened the container, dumped the frozen lump of soup into a pot. She'd made the chicken noodle for a church soup-and-sandwich meal, but she'd decided at the last minute not to go. She hadn't wanted to sit at a table filled with single men and women who all seemed to want nothing more than to find their soul mates.

All *she* wanted was to find some peace, but that was as elusive as mountain mist.

"I'll call her myself. See if we can get some answers for a change." Andrew sighed. "I'd better head out. I'm going to have to take the photos as evidence, Raina. I can't promise that you'll get them back."

"It's okay." But it wasn't really. Now that she'd seen the photographs, she wanted them desperately. Which was silly. She had plenty of pictures in her bedroom and tucked away in photo albums in her closet. She didn't need two more. Especially two with the faces scratched out of them. Still, sending them with Andrew felt like sending away a piece of her heart.

"I'll call as soon as I know something. In the meantime, stay safe. No more going for walks without an escort."

"I won't."

"Don't say it if you don't mean it, okay?" Andrew's gaze was sharp, his expression hard. "I don't like the way things are playing out, and if you're not careful, what happened to Butch will happen to you."

It sounded more like a threat than a warning, and Raina's skin crawled. She touched her throat. It didn't take much to crush a windpipe. A little more pressure and the guy who'd attacked her could have done it easily.

"I'm heading out." Andrew nodded curtly, no humor, no kindness, no compassion in his gaze, just that same implacable expression. "You have my cell phone number. Call immediately if anything happens."

"Do you want me to—"

"I want you to stay in this house behind closed doors until this is over. That's *all* I want you to do," he snapped.

He stalked from the room, brisk footsteps tapping on the floor, the front door opening and then shutting with a little too much force.

"Guy has a temper on him," Boone commented, pulling another cookie from the package.

"How well do you know him, Raina?" Jackson's brother asked.

"Really well. I've known him since we were kids. After I got married, he and my husband were good friends."

"I see." Chance crossed his arms over his chest, his expression unreadable.

Raina didn't know what he saw, but she had a feeling it wasn't anything good. "If you're thinking that Andrew has something to do with the trouble I've been having, you're thinking wrong."

"At the moment, I'm not thinking anything. Except that someone did a number on your head." His gaze dropped to her throat, and she resisted the urge to touch the bruises she knew were there. "And your throat. A little more pressure, and you'd be dead."

Exactly what she'd been thinking, but she wasn't going to admit it to Chance.

"Ignore my brother, Raina," Jackson cut in. "He gets grumpy when things are out of his control."

"I get grumpy," Chance ground out, "when my brother gets questioned by the police."

"I think we've covered this before," Boone said. "How about we skip the replay and have some of whatever is in that pot? It smells great."

He leaned in close, inhaled deeply.

Raina couldn't help smiling. He was good-looking, laid-back and a lot easier on the emotions than Jackson. "It's homemade chicken noodle soup."

"What kind of noodles?"

"Egg."

"You put carrots in it?"

"And celery. Roasted chicken and some seasoning. It's my grandmother's recipe. Passed down for three generations."

He whistled softly. "I think I'm in love with your grandmother."

"You haven't even tasted the soup yet." She laughed.

"But I will, and once I do, I'm going to be smitten. It's just the way it is."

"My grandmother will be flattered, but since she's been married for sixty years, your love is going to be unrequited."

"Maybe I can convince her to adopt me, then." He grabbed a spoon from the drying rack and dipped it into the stone-cold soup.

"It's still half-frozen!" she protested, but he scooped a spoonful into his mouth and sighed blissfully.

"Yep," he said. "Love. Just pour about half of that in a bowl for me. You and the brothers can share the rest."

"Selfish a little?" Chance asked, but even he seemed amused by Boone.

"Hungry a lot. Seeing as how that's mostly your fault for sending me off without enough cash to adequately nourish my body—"

"You had plenty of money," Chance protested.

Raina smiled, enjoying the banter and the obvious camaraderie between the men.

"The soup will be ready in a few minutes," she interrupted. "If you want to grab sheets and blankets in the linen closet in the hall while you're waiting, you can make up some beds on the couch. I'd offer beds, but I don't have any spares."

"There's no need for that," Chance said, his smooth baritone nothing like his brother's deep Southern drawl. Despite the soot that stained his dress shirt, he looked polished and put together, his black slacks pressed, his wool coat a deep black with no sign of fading or wear and tear. A shoulder holster peeked out from beneath the coat, but the gun remained hidden. He might look more polished, but Raina had a feeling he was just as tough as his brother. "Boone and I aren't planning to stay."

"We're not planning to drive all the way back to D.C., either," Boone mumbled through a mouthful of cookie.

Chance frowned. "You have a better idea?"

"Yeah. We take the lady up on her offer, make beds for ourselves and sleep until the sun comes up. I, for one, could use a little shut-eye."

"You can sleep in the car."

"You're not hearing me, Chance," Boone said. "I don't want to drive, fly or jog anywhere tonight. After all the travel I've been doing for the company the past few months, all I want to do is lie down. Doesn't matter if I'm lying down on a bed, rocks, a ledge or the floor, as long as I get to sleep and no one disturbs me." He closed the package of cookies and wiped crumbs from his shirt.

Raina stirred the soup and let the conversation wash over her. It felt nice, the words filling the room in a way nothing had in the past few months. It wasn't just the men's physical presence. It was their energy, their obvious connection and fondness for one another. They were family, and that made the house feel like a home.

She hadn't realized how much she'd missed that until it was there again—the warmth, the joy, the simple pleasure of being together.

She grabbed a spoon from the drainer near the sink, her eyes burning, her chest tight. Life was moving on. *She* was moving on. She felt that more than she ever had, felt the slow shifting of focus from the past to the future.

It was the way it should be, but it still hurt, because moving on meant letting go, and she didn't know how she could ever do that.

She turned on the water, rinsed the already clean spoon because she didn't want the men to see the tears in her eyes.

Something moved in the window above the sink. A face, pressing against the glass, skin white, eyes as black as the deepest darkness.

She screamed, stumbled back.

Screamed again as the lights went out and the kitchen plunged into darkness.

# FIFTEEN

Jackson sprinted to the back door, adrenaline surging through him. Someone had been staring in the window. He'd seen the face, turned off the light to keep whoever it was from having a clear view of the interior.

"Boone, stay with the lady," Chance barked, coming up on Jackson's heels.

They hit the edge of the back deck at the same time, pausing in unison, a team, ready to work together, fight together, do whatever it took to succeed together. They had their differences, but when it came to the job, they were always absolutely in sync.

"Be careful, bro," Chance muttered. "I don't want you taken out by some small-town thug who has a crush on your lady friend."

"You be careful, too," Jackson responded. "Mom would ki…"

His voice trailed off as he caught sight of a

dark figure moving slowly toward the corner of the house. *Very* slowly.

He touched his brother's arm, gestured to what looked to be an ancient man. White hair, white nightshirt tucked into baggy black sweats.

*A disguise,* Chance mouthed, but Jackson didn't think so. The guy moved as if every bone in his body hurt, his feet shuffling through dry grass as he picked his way across the yard. If he was trying to make an escape, he wasn't doing it very effectively.

"Sir!" Jackson called out, and the old guy paused, glancing over his shoulder and scowling.

"Go back to whatever shenanigans you were up to," he spat. "I'm going home to call the cops."

"I'd say the shenanigans are more on your part," Chance responded. "Peeking into other people's windows is a crime."

"She's not other people, son. She's my neighbor. I have an obligation to check on her when every light in the house is on and cars are filling up the driveway," the man snapped. "Too many people on this road lately. That's the problem, and you can rest assured, I'm going to let the police know about it."

"Larry?" Raina peered out the open door, her face a pale oval in the darkness. "Is that you?"

"Who else would it be? Now, like I said, you

just go on back to what you were doing." He started shuffling away again, but Raina hurried onto the deck, probably would have gone after the guy if Jackson hadn't grabbed her belt loop and pulled her to a stop.

"I'm making chicken noodle soup, Larry. Come on in and have some before you go home."

"Come into your den of iniquity? I don't think so." But Larry stopped again, gnarled fists settling on his narrow hips. "What would Matt think? That's what I want to know? A Christian woman like you with three grown men in her house."

"There's a woman here, too," Raina responded, pulling at Jackson's fingers and trying to loosen his grip on her belt loop.

Wasn't going to happen. Larry might be old, but that didn't mean he wasn't responsible for Raina's troubles.

"And that makes it better?" Larry huffed, shuffling back toward them, his slow plodding movements almost painful to watch.

He made it to the steps, and Chance took his arm, helping him onto the deck. "Sir, I think you're misunderstanding the situation."

"What's to misunderstand? A beautiful young widow and three men who are taking advantage of her grief. I'd say I'm not misunderstanding a thing!"

"Actually, Larry," Raina said, "these men are from HEART. The organization that rescued me from—"

"I know where you were rescued from, Raina. It was all over the news," Larry snapped.

"If you're following the news, then you've probably seen the stories about my efforts to—"

"Bring a kid over here. Yeah. Yeah. I've seen it. What does that have to do with the price of tea in China?"

"Everything," Raina responded with a lot more patience than Jackson was feeling. "Samuel's flight got canceled because of the storm we had. Jackson and a coworker drove him here."

"And now they're all staying the night? You think that's appropriate?"

"Yes, actually," Raina said kindly. "I do. We aren't supposed to turn away strangers who are in need. Why would we turn away people that we know?" She took Larry's arm, led him into the kitchen.

The light was already on, and Boone was standing over the soup pot, several bowls on the counter beside him. "Looked like things were under control, so I thought I'd keep the food from burning."

"Good to see your priorities are right." Chance sighed, dropping into one of the kitchen chairs. He looked worn, the fine lines near his eyes deeper.

"Go ahead and have a seat, Larry." Raina pulled out another chair. "I made my grandmother's chicken noodle soup."

"Can't be better than Dora's," Larry muttered, but he eased into the chair, his bones creaking.

"Dora?" Boone asked, spooning soup into a bowl and setting it on the table in front of Larry.

"My late wife. May God rest her soul." Larry took the spoon that Raina handed him and dug into the soup with more gusto than Jackson expected. From the way he was eating, Jackson would say he hadn't had a meal in a while.

Raina must have been thinking the same thing. She frowned and opened an old-fashioned bread box that sat on the counter. "How about some bread with that, Larry?"

"I wouldn't want to impose," he said, but he took the slice she offered him, layering it with cold butter Raina took from the fridge.

"You want some?" Boone asked, pointing the serving spoon in Jackson's direction.

"No. Thanks."

"Suit yourself. Me? I'm going to eat seconds."

"When did you have firsts?" Chance looked up from the bowl Boone had set in front of him.

"While the ol—" He glanced at Larry. "While Larry was heading back across the yard. Took him a while and that was just enough time for me to eat soup."

"I've got old bones, kid. You don't understand because you're young and healthy, but just you wait. Your turn is coming, and you'll be the one shuffling across a yard you used to do backflips in."

"Good to know," Boone said without ire. He had the patience of a saint. "Want some more soup?"

"I think I will." Larry held out his bowl. "It's good soup, Raina. Not Dora good, but good enough to eat more."

"Thanks, Larry." She smiled, her eyes red-rimmed and deeply shadowed. "I'm making another batch tomorrow. I'll bring some over for you."

Jackson doubted that making soup had really been on her agenda for the day, but Larry's collarbone was prominent above the neckline of his nightshirt, his cheeks hollow. He either didn't have money for food or didn't bother eating. Either way, he needed to be fed.

He handed the guy another slice of bread.

"You said there's been too many people on this road lately, Larry. What did you mean?"

"All kinds of cars driving up and down the road."

"You mean the cars that are in the driveway?" he pressed, because the guy might be thin and ornery, but his eyes seemed to be working just fine. If he'd seen something or someone skulking around the house, Jackson wanted to know it.

"Do you think I'm dense, son?" Larry retorted. "The police car drove away ten minutes ago. Five minutes after that, a car drove down to the end of the road, did a U-turn and left again. That's when I decided enough was enough."

"Did you see what the car looked like?"

"Black. A sporty little sedan. Not an American-made car. Some foreign model." Larry sniffed. "You'd think people would want to support their own country's economy, but that's the kind of world we live in. Everyone for them—"

"Have you seen the car around here before?" Chance cut him off, obviously trying to keep the conversation on track.

"I can't say that I have." Larry frowned, dipping buttered bread into his soup and letting the broth drip down his chin as he ate it. "Of course—" he grabbed a napkin from a holder that sat in the middle of the table and wiped his chin "—I haven't seen the Jeep in a couple of nights, so maybe the guy got a new car."

"What Jeep?" Raina asked.

"How should I know what Jeep? All I know is that it's been coming around here for a few months."

Jackson's pulse jumped, and he met Raina's eyes. "Are you sure you don't know anyone besides Destiny's boyfriend who owns a Jeep?"

She bit her lip, shook her head. "No."

"Well, someone with a Jeep knows you," Larry replied. "Guy drives down this road once or twice a week. I almost called the cops a few times, but they threatened to haul me in for criminal mischief if I made any more false reports. Not that my reports were false. My church shoes didn't just disappear from my closet and reappear in my bedroom all by themselves, and someone *did* steal my lunch one day. I made that sandwich as sure as I'm sitting at this table eating pork roast."

No one pointed out that he was eating chicken noodle soup.

"What color was the Jeep?" Jackson asked, not sure if Larry had really seen the Jeep or if he'd imagined it the way he'd imagined the pork in his bowl.

"Blue. Not one of those fancy Jeeps, either. An old one. Had a couple of dents in the fender.

This guy is smart. Values his dollars." Larry nodded his head vigorously, his white hair flopping over his eyes.

"Is that the color of the Jeep they found abandoned earlier?" Chance asked.

"Yeah," Jackson responded, and it fit the description perfectly. If Larry was right about what he'd seen, someone had been stalking Raina for longer than a few days.

"Did you happen to see the driver, Larry?"

"Never got a good look at the guy. He did get out once. Walked up to Raina's front window and looked inside. The lights were on, but I knew she wasn't home, so I wasn't worried about him being some pervert. I thought maybe he was scoping the house out, trying to see if she had anything he could steal. Good thing Matt was a pastor and not a multimillionaire." He let out a bark of laughter that ended in a dry, raspy cough.

Raina set a glass of water near his elbow. "When was that, Larry? You never mentioned it to me before."

"A year or two ago?" Larry frowned, sopping up the last bit of soup with a third piece of bread. "And I didn't mention it because I didn't want to scare you. I've been watching, keeping old Bessie real close."

"Bessie?"

"My hunting rifle." He glanced around the

room. "I guess I forgot to grab her on my way out the door."

"Thank the good Lord for that," Boone murmured.

"What's that?" Larry speared him with a hard look.

"You mentioned that you'd been seeing the Jeep for a few months," Boone said, sidestepping the question. "Not a few years. So how is it possible you saw the guy a couple of years ago?"

"Did I say a couple of years?" Larry rubbed his forehead, his knuckles knotted with arthritis. "That was a mistake. The guy hasn't been coming out that long. You call the police. They'll tell you what day it was. I called them and left a message for that Eric guy. I knew he was your friend, Raina, so I thought he'd take it seriously."

"You mean Andrew Wallace?" Raina asked.

"Yes. Right. Andrew. I don't know what it is with me and names lately." He stood carefully, as if every movement hurt. "The thing is, I told Matt that if anything happened to him, I'd take care of you and the kid. I can't take care of the kid, but I can look out for you. Unfortunately, that dingbat cop didn't even bother to come out to investigate."

"Thanks for trying," Raina said.

"Don't thank me. Thank that husband of yours, when you see him on the other side." He paused with his hand on the front doorknob, his shoulders slumped beneath his baggy nightshirt. "Matt is the only person who ever understood about me and Dora, and I owe him big for that."

"What did he understand about her?" Raina asked gently, and Jackson braced himself for the answer, because he knew it was going to cut deep, make him think about all the things that were possible when two people loved each other enough to make things work.

"That when she died, she took a piece of me with her. I never did get that piece back. No matter how many years passed. Three decades, and she's still the only person I want to be around. Most people don't get that, but Matt did." He blinked rheumy eyes. "And you know, it was mighty nice having someone care about me for a while."

He opened the door, and Boone hurried after him, a heavy winter coat in his arms. "Hey, Pops! It's too cold to be outside without a coat."

"Who you calling Pops, boy?"

"It's what I call my grandfather."

Larry snorted, but he didn't shove away the coat Boone slung around his shoulders.

"Would you like it better if I called you 'old man'?" Boone put a hand on Larry's elbow and the two made their way down the stairs, whatever Larry said in reply was lost in the rustling of the trees.

"I should probably go with them," Raina said, more to herself than anyone else.

"Boone will take care of him." Jackson tugged her away from the open door and the chilly night air. "And I'm thinking it's not the best idea for you to be outside."

"He's right," Chance said. "If someone drove by the house after Officer Wallace left, we could be dealing with a stalker who's so deeply enmeshed in his fantasies, he doesn't care if he's seen. At the very least, we're dealing with someone who's keeping an eye on the house, who knows when Raina is home and when she's gone."

"The question is, what does he want?" Jackson asked the question that was floating around in Raina's head.

"Love? Attention?" Chance suggested. "He's a crackpot, so it's hard to say. I'm going to drive down the road, see if anyone is parked close by. I'll call Wallace on the way. Make sure he's updated on everything. Try not to get in any trouble while I'm gone, Jackson." He walked outside and shut the door, leaving a cool gust of wind and sudden silence in his wake.

"Do you think Chance is right about the person wanting love and affection? Do you actually think someone has been stalking me for months?" Raina finally asked, because she was hoping that he didn't.

"I don't know. Larry seems confused, but he was pretty clear on the details of that Jeep. It sounded just like the one that the police impounded at your in-laws' old house today. Which looked like the one that nearly ran me down. That's two vehicles. If Larry is right about the sedan, that's three. Could be our guy has multiple vehicles to keep from being noticed when he's following you."

"If he's following me."

"Don't bury your head in the sand, Raina. Something is going on here, and it all revolves around you."

"I know. That's what worries me."

"You don't have to worry, Raina. You have people who care about you and a God who's bigger than all your problems."

"I know, but it's still hard sometimes." She rubbed her arms, trying to chase away the chill that seemed to had sunk so deep into her bones that she didn't think it would ever leave.

"What's hard?" he asked, cupping her shoulders, looking into her face.

He was nothing like Matt. Not quiet or easy or bookish. If he had been, it would have been so much easier to explain what she felt when she looked into his eyes.

"This is hard," she breathed, her throat tight and hot from emotions she didn't want to feel. "Moving on. Letting go. It's hard."

"The other option is being like Larry. Bitter and lonely and angry at the world and at God."

"I'm not angry. I'm confused." She moved to the fireplace, putting some distance between Jackson and herself so she could think. "I thought I was doing it right, making good choices, following the path God wanted me on. Then the rug got pulled out from under me and—"

"You wondered if you'd made a mistake somewhere along the line. If maybe you were being punished for not being the Christian God wanted you to be?"

"Yes. I guess so," she admitted.

"It's a game our minds play, Raina, to help us make sense of the incomprehensible. But it doesn't speak to the truth." He touched her cheek, his fingers sliding to her nape, kneading the tense muscles there.

"What is the truth, then, Jackson?" she murmured. "That things just happen? That tragedy is all around us, and we just have to make the best of it?"

"That God's love prevails. Even in the darkest times. Even when we lose everything." He tugged her closer, his palm warm on her neck, his eyes midnight-blue and filled with sincerity and compassion. "That faith is something that grows during trials and that holding on to it leads us to the exact place where we belong."

*Like here with you?* she wanted to ask, but he leaned in, his lips brushing her temple, her cheek, her lips, and all the tears she hadn't wanted to cry were suddenly there, in her eyes, on her cheeks, dripping down her chin.

"Shh." He wrapped his arms around her. "It's going to be okay."

She could have moved away.

It should have been easy to, but she felt drugged by his touch, her muscles relaxing for the first time in what seemed like months. And instead of moving away, she stayed right where she was, her hands on his waist, her head resting against his chest while the clock ticked away the minutes and the wind began to howl beneath the eaves.

# SIXTEEN

She woke to the sound of a child crying. Not the frantic cries of her nightmares. The quiet sniffles of someone who didn't want to be heard.

She sat up, cocked her head to the side. Rain splattered against the window, another round of icy storms moving in. The wind buffeted the glass and sent sheets of rain splattering against the siding, its quiet moan an eerie backdrop to the rain.

Was that what had woken her?

No. There it was again! Just below the sound of the storm. A quiet sob.

Samuel?

It had to be. She climbed out of bed, yanked a robe on over her flannel pajamas and crept into the hallway. Boone and Chance were sleeping in the living room, the soft glow of the fire she'd lit for them undulating on the floor at the head of the hall.

Samuel's door was open, his muffled sobs drifting into the hall.

"Samuel?" she whispered from the doorway.

The cries stopped, but he didn't respond.

She walked into the dark room, nearly tripping over Samuel's backpack. He'd crumpled it up, spilled all the contents onto the floor. She flipped on the light, stepping over the mess and walking to the bed. He had the pillow over his head, one thin hand pressing it close to his ear.

"Samuel?" She touched his shoulder, felt him trembling.

She almost backed away, almost left him there because it seemed like what he wanted. But he was a child with wounds so deep, she wasn't sure they would ever heal. *Knew* they never would if someone didn't care enough to hold out a hand and pull him close, to tell him that things would get better.

She tugged on the pillow, and he released it, rolling onto his back and staring at the ceiling, his cheeks wet with tears. A picture was on the bed beside him, the grainy color photo smudged with dirt, one edge ripped off. She knew it was his family. Mother, father, a teenage sister, a toddler. He was there, too, much younger, but she recognized his wide brown eyes and thick lashes.

"It's hard when you miss someone, isn't it?"

she asked quietly, and he opened his mouth, let out a mournful cry. It broke Raina's heart in a hundred ways it had never been broken before, and she reached for him. She pulled him onto her lap even though he wasn't a baby, wasn't her son, probably hadn't been held by anyone in so many years that he'd forgotten what it was like.

"I'm sorry, Samuel," she whispered against his ear. "I wish I could bring them back to you, but I can't. I can only give you what I have here."

"Until one year," he wailed. "And I will be alone again."

She winced at his words. That's the way it had been planned. A year of medical help, of therapy, of healing his body and mind. She'd been hoping and praying that someone would step forward before Samuel's visa expired, but there was no guarantee. She couldn't let him go back, though. She knew that now, had probably always known it. He deserved more, needed more, and if she didn't give it to him, she couldn't count on anyone else doing it.

"No. You won't," she said, because she couldn't tell him anything else. "We'll work things out, Samuel. I promise. We'll make sure you can stay."

He shook his head, eased off her lap, a little boy who looked like an old man, his eyes too filled with weariness.

"No," he said. "You have had your son, and he is gone. You do not need another son."

"I do not need another son like the one I had. There can only ever be one of him," she said honestly. "But I need someone. My house is too empty now that my family is gone."

"My heart is empty." He touched his chest, and Raina's heart shattered again.

"Maybe we both need help filling the empty places. Come on. Let's take your family photo and put it in a frame so that it won't be ruined." She offered a hand, and he took it.

"What is a frame?"

"Something to put photos in. With glass and plastic or wood around the edges. Like that." She pointed to a picture of a cartoon frog that she'd framed and hung on the wall.

Samuel nodded and reached for the family photo, holding it tenderly. She handed him a crutch and he positioned it under his arm, the picture so carefully held that it might have been the finest china or the most valuable jewel.

She had plenty of framed photos in her room, and she brought him there, lifting one off the dresser. Matt smiled out at her, his dark eyes filled with amusement. She remembered taking the picture. They'd been hiking on the Appalachian Trail a few months before Joseph's birth, the fall foliage thick and beautiful.

Her heart ached as she looked at it, but she slid it from the frame, placed it in a drawer that used to be filled with Matt's T-shirts, but had been empty for almost as long as he'd been gone. When she closed the drawer, it felt like saying another goodbye.

"Okay," she said, her voice just a little shaky. "Let's do this."

She helped Joseph slide the photo into place, showed him how to close the back, then flipped it over and handed it to him. "There. Now it will be protected. You can put it on the dresser in your room. After your infection is gone, we'll go to the store and have copies of it made."

"Thank you." He stared down at the photo, then set it on the dresser next to a picture that had been taken at the church picnic four months before the accident. She and Matt sitting in the shade of an elm tree, Joseph standing behind them, his arms around both of their shoulders. "There," Samuel said. "Now we are all family."

She nodded, because she couldn't speak, didn't even know what to say. She'd gone to Africa because she'd needed to escape her heartache and because she'd wanted to renew her faith. She'd thought she would give plenty and expected to get nothing in return.

She'd gotten Samuel, though. A boy who'd risked everything to save her life. The least she could do was risk her heart to give him what he needed the most. "Yes," she agreed. "We are all family. Now you need to get back in bed. Your infection won't heal if you don't get the rest you need."

He didn't argue, just hopped back to his room and climbed into bed. Raina pulled the covers over him, kissed his forehead, touched his cheek. "Sleep well, Samuel."

"Sleep well, Raina, and have the sweetest dreams," he replied. "Good night."

She turned off the light, left the door open and walked back to her room. It was nearly three in the morning, but she didn't think she could sleep. If she hadn't had guests, she'd have gone into the living room, sat in front of the fire, lost herself in a movie or a good book.

She paced to the window that overlooked the backyard. The wind whistled through the trees, scattering dead leaves across the ground. It gusted through the single pane glass, and she shivered. It looked bitterly cold out, but she'd rather be sitting on the back deck than be cooped up in her room. She touched the lock on the window, thought about how easy it would be to open it up and climb out into the whipping wind. Thought about just how foolish that would be.

"I thought I heard you moving around in here. You're not planning to make your escape, are you?" Jackson said quietly, his voice so surprising, she jumped.

"Good gravy!" she snapped. "You scared me."

"'Good gravy'?" He laughed, stepping farther into the room, his body silhouetted by the light filtering down the hall from the living room. Broad shoulders, slim hips, a laugh that made her want to smile. If she'd met him before Matt, she'd have been smitten from the first moment she'd looked into his eyes.

But she'd met him after, and she still couldn't seem to resist.

"You sound like my great-grandmother," he continued. "One of the most interesting Southern belles in all of Raleigh. The woman did have a way with words. She still does."

"I think I'd like your great-grandmother."

"Then you'll have to meet her. She's coming to D.C. for Thanksgiving. Might be hard to fit her and the rest of the Miller clan in my apartment, but I'll manage. If someone doesn't offer me a bigger space. Like a house. On some acreage."

"Is that a hint?" she asked with a smile.

"No hint, Raina. It's a blatant attempt to secure your premises for the occasion," he responded, his Southern drawl so thick, she laughed.

"Are you trying to charm me into it, Jackson?" Because it was working, and she didn't think she minded at all.

"Just trying to get what I need. Chance and I were supposed to host the meal at his place, but he burned his house down in an attempt to get out of it."

"He burned his own house down?"

"I should rephrase that. His faulty furnace exploded and burned the house down. He's homeless and living at the HEART offices for the next few months."

"Why not with you?"

"I live in a one-bedroom apartment the size of a postage stamp. He stayed three nights and decided he needed a little more room to breathe. His new house should be ready to move into by Christmas. In the meantime, I have the whole Thanksgiving dilemma to deal with. I need help, and I'm not afraid to ask for it."

She almost said no. She'd spent the past three Thanksgivings at her parents', having quiet meals where no mention was made of the people who were missing. It wasn't special or fun, but it was what she did, and it had become as comfortable as an old pair of shoes.

The thing was, she didn't really want comfort anymore. She wanted the little thrill of excitement that came from looking to the future, imagining new and wonderful things. If Matt were standing behind her, whispering in her ear, he'd tell her that was the way things should be. "You may not be afraid to ask," she said. "But I'm kind of afraid to give it. Your family sounds…"

"Intimidating? Scary? Overwhelming? Loud? Those are all apt descriptions. And the truth is, my family is a little nuts, but they're great people."

"You don't have to convince me. I'll help you out."

"Seriously?"

"Yes. I'll even make peach pie to go with the pumpkin and apple."

"You make the peach. We've got plenty of people in the family who will bring the others."

"How many are we talking about?" she asked.

"A dozen. Two. It's hard to tell. Lots of uncles and aunts and cousins. Stella usually comes, but I think that might not happen this time." He didn't explain why, and she didn't ask. She'd sensed tension between Stella and Chance, and she figured it had something to do with that.

"I should probably invite Larry."

"I think you should."

"And Destiny."

"And the good doctor Kent?" he asked, closing the distance between them. She could see his face in the darkness, the hard angle of his jaw, the sharp edge of his cheekbone, the smooth firm line of his lips. He'd changed into a shirt that looked like a blue version of his brother's, only he hadn't tucked it into jeans that were a shade darker than the ones he'd been wearing earlier.

"I think he'll be busy working at the soup kitchen."

"What if he isn't?"

"I'm sure he'll have plenty of invitations to choose from. Even if he doesn't, I'm not planning to invite him. I wouldn't want to lead him on. He's not my type, and it wouldn't be fair to make him think he is."

"So, if he's not your type, who is?" He smoothed his palms up her arms, his hands settling on her shoulders.

She wasn't sure how to answer. Ten years ago, her type had been bookish and quiet, funny and smart, caring and just a little awkward. She was beginning to realize she had a soft spot for tall, dark-haired men with Southern accents.

It shouldn't have made her sad, but it did.

She swallowed down the lump of grief, tried to make herself smile. "I don't know. It's been a long time since I've thought about it."

"Maybe you could think about it," Jackson responded, his fingers playing in the ends of her hair. "And let me know after this is all over."

"*If* it's ever over."

"It will be. Trouble never lasts forever."

He was right. It didn't. Maybe heartache

didn't, either. Maybe, after enough time passed, wounds healed and hearts mended and lives that were empty could be filled again.

A soft buzzing sound filled the room, and she frowned. "What's that?"

"My cell phone." He dug it from his pocket, glanced at the number. "It's Wallace. I'd better take it."

She switched on the light while he answered, perched on the bed while he listened. It wasn't good news. She could tell by the hardness in his eyes, the tightness in his jaw.

"Are you sure?" he finally asked. "Okay. Will do. Thanks."

He tucked the phone back in his pocket.

"What's going on?" she asked, following him as he walked into the hall.

"The evidence team found a scarf in the back of the Jeep that nearly ran me down. Fibers on it matched fibers that were clinging to Butch's coat when he was found."

The news was like a splash of ice water in the face, every thought of Thanksgiving and moving on fading in the wake of it. "So he was murdered by the person who's stalking me," she said.

"It looks that way."

He walked into the living room. She waited in the threshold, afraid to walk in on the men who were sleeping.

"Might as well come in," Boone called. "We're decent, and thanks to Jackson, we're awake."

She stepped into the living room, the firelight casting a warm glow over the room. She'd forgotten how nice it was to have the fire burning, the room toasty, the logs snapping.

Boone stood near the fireplace, his red hair fiery in the light. "I guess neither of you know the first thing about jet lag. If you did, you wouldn't wake a man who just got back from the Middle East."

"Sorry, Boone," Jackson said, and he didn't sound sorry at all. "But we've got a situation, and I need to fill you in on it."

"What situation?" Chance asked. At some point, he'd changed into a brick red T-shirt and faded jeans. Even in those, he looked polished.

"Hold on," Boone said. "If we're going to be briefed, we may as well get Stella involved. Otherwise, she'll show up right around the time I'm falling asleep again and want the information."

"Someone can fill her in in the morning," Chance said, stalking to the switch on the wall and turning it on. "Now, what's going on, Jackson?"

"Hold on, boss." Boone straightened to his full height and crossed his arms over his chest. For the first time since Raina had met him, he looked angry and just a little dangerous. "We don't break the rules for anyone. Not even for you, and the team rules are that everyone on a mission is present during the briefing."

"This isn't a mission," Chance growled.

"Yeah. It is. You set up the parameters of what a mission was way before the company executed its first rescue. Once we commit to helping someone, we're on mission together until the job is done. Doesn't matter if we're getting paid."

"Now you remember the rules?" Chance sighed. "Fine. Someone go get her. Then Jackson will brief us. Happy?"

"Does a whip-poor-will sing in the morning?" Boone responded.

"I don't know, Boone. How about you just go get Stella, so we can move on with things?" Chance growled.

"I will." He snagged Raina's hand as he walked by, pulling her toward the kitchen. "And maybe you can make some coffee for us, Raina?"

"Sure," she said, more worried about what else Jackson was going to say than coffee, missions or rules.

"And maybe an omelet? Some toast? Nothing fancy. Just something to keep the brain working."

"I can do that," she said, opening the fridge and pulling out what she needed.

"You're a good kid," he responded, ruffling

her hair. "I like you. I think you and Jackson are going to do just fine together."

He disappeared upstairs, and she started the coffeepot, cracked eggs into a bowl, put bread in the toaster. Went through all the motions of making breakfast for the team who was protecting her, and the whole time, his words were running through her head.

*I think you and Jackson are going to do just fine together.*

A few days ago, she would have laughed at the idea that she could be fine with anyone.

She wasn't laughing anymore.

She was praying, hoping, believing that there was something good coming out of the bad, and that Jackson was right. That her troubles wouldn't last forever, that when they were over, she'd have Thanksgiving with his rowdy family and with Samuel, and all the things she'd believed about God and faith and hope, all the things she'd thought she'd lost when Joseph and Matt died, would finally be renewed.

# SEVENTEEN

At ten-thirty in the morning, Raina had already run out of ideas for entertaining Samuel. Being stuck in the house wasn't fun, especially for a ten-year-old boy. Unfortunately, aside from a visit to the doctor, Raina and Samuel had been confined to the house. Thank goodness Samuel had another appointment scheduled for that afternoon. They both needed to get outside, get a little fresh air, try to move beyond the circumstances they were in.

Not easy to do when the circumstances never seemed to change. After nearly a week of investigating, the police were no closer to finding Butch's murderer. Which meant, of course, that they were no closer to finding Raina's stalker. Things had been so quiet for the past few days, Raina was beginning to wonder if there'd ever actually been a stalker. If not for the healing wound on her forehead and the fading bruises on her neck, she could almost believe there wasn't one.

Raina sighed, shoving her hands into soapy dishwater and pulling out a plate. She scrubbed it, rinsed it and handed it to Samuel.

"I can wash these," he offered. "You rest."

"It will be faster if we work together. When we're done, we can play chess." After nearly a week of spending almost all their time together, she'd learned a lot about Samuel. He loved learning. He loved games that made him think, television shows that taught him something. He could read quite a bit of English, and he loved books. He also liked to help, and he treated her like an elderly aunt who might expire at any moment if she didn't get enough rest. Sometimes that made her smile. Other times it made her wonder if she should slap on some foundation and blush and try to look a little younger.

The floorboards above her head creaked as she handed Samuel another plate to dry. Jackson was upstairs with Stella and Boone. Chance was in the living room on Skype with a team member who was in China. It seemed strange that a house that had been empty and lonely for years was suddenly full. That meant more dishes, more cooking, more cleaning. It also meant more companionship. Raina hadn't realized how much she'd missed that until she suddenly had it again.

"I was thinking," she said as she washed the

last dish and pulled the plug. "After we go to the doctor today, we should stop at the library and get some books."

"Library?" Samuel wiped the last drop of water from the dish and carefully set it on the counter.

"It's a place where you can go and borrow books. Once you read the books, you return them and you can borrow more."

"Really?" His dark eyes lit up, a smile spreading across his face. "I think I will like a library."

"Who's going to the library?" Jackson walked into the room wearing what looked like another one of his brother's dress shirts. This one was a deep blue that matched his eyes, the fabric soft and well-worn. He'd rolled the sleeves up to his elbows and left the buttons undone, a dove-gray T-shirt beneath clinging to his chest and abdomen. His muscles were clearly defined, the holster he wore strapped to his chest emphasizing his masculinity.

Her heart jumped as he walked toward her, her stomach filling with a million butterflies. Being near him was like the first day of summer, warm and exciting and wonderful with just a hint of regret because spring was over.

"I thought I could take Samuel there after his doctor's appointment," she responded, hoping he didn't notice how flushed her skin was.

She felt like a schoolgirl with a crush, awkward and unsure.

"Since when did he have a doctor's appointment today?" Jackson asked, snagging an apple from a basket of fruit Destiny had dropped off the day before.

"Since before he arrived. We're having X-rays done to see how the bone in his leg looks. The prosthesis can't be fitted until it's healed completely. I told Stella about it."

"Stella didn't tell me," he said with a frown. "This is going to be at the clinic?"

"No. We're going to River Valley Radiology. It's in the same building as the clinic, but not in the same offices."

"Good."

"What's good about it?"

"I don't like Kent," he said bluntly.

"Don't like whom?" Chance walked into the room, his shirt neatly pressed, a tie hanging loosely around his neck. He spent most of his time on the computer or on the phone, but when he wasn't occupied with work, he was kind to Samuel, offering to play board games and read books with him. That meant a lot to Raina, because she could tell it meant a lot to Samuel. He craved love and attention the way plants craved sunlight, needed it the way he needed to breathe.

"Kent Moreland. The guy makes my blood

boil." And Jackson wasn't going to apologize for it. The guy called every day. He always had a reason. He wanted to check on Samuel or find out if Raina planned to return to work as scheduled or tell her that one of her coworkers had had a baby girl.

"Is he a person of interest in the case?" Leave it to Chance to get to the point and to the problem. No matter what Jackson's gut said, there was no evidence against Kent, nothing to make the police bring him in for questioning.

"No."

"Of course not!" Raina frowned. Her cheeks were flushed, her eyes glowing blue-purple, the small bandage that covered the wound on her forehead stark white. She looked young and pretty and too vulnerable for Jackson's peace of mind.

"I'm just asking," Chance responded, meeting Jackson's eyes. "I figured Jackson had some reason for not liking the guy. I thought it might have to do with the case."

"They butt heads," Raina responded, but that wasn't all there was to it, and Jackson thought she knew it.

"It's more than that," Jackson said. "The guy is pompous. He thinks he's better than the average Joe, and as far as he's concerned everyone but him is average."

"In other words," Chance replied, "he's interested in Raina and you don't like it?"

Raina blushed, but Jackson wasn't going to deny the truth. "There's that, too."

"What's Wallace have to say about the guy?"

"He's looking into Kent's background because I asked him to."

"What?" Raina frowned. "Why would you do that?"

"Because I don't trust him, and usually, I'm spot-on about people."

"It's true," Chance agreed. "But I think our better bet for a suspect is Lucas Raymond. I did a little research of my own, and he's been MIA for three days. Canceled his appointments, asked a neighbor to feed his cat."

Chance took a seat at the kitchen table, his gaze on Samuel. The kid had stacked clean plates on the counter and was putting dry silverware into a drawer, carefully arranging it by size and style. Jackson thought that probably amused his brother. Like Samuel, Chance loved organization and order.

"I can top the MIA psychiatrist," Jackson said. "Kent's wife committed suicide."

"Really?" Raina looked shocked. "He told me that she died in a car accident."

"She did. If you count sealing the car muffler, closing the car windows and running the engine until you succumb to carbon monoxide poisoning an accident." It had taken Jackson a couple of days to track down the information, but he'd finally managed to contact someone in Kent's Wisconsin hometown who was willing to talk about Cheryl Moreland's death.

"That's horrible," Raina said, her gaze jumping to Samuel. He'd finished with the silverware and was wiping off the counter. "And it may not be good subject matter for a ten-year-old boy."

She was right about that. Samuel didn't need any more sad stories in his life. He didn't need any more loss or heartache. Raina wasn't the only one Jackson was bent on protecting.

"Hey, buddy." Jackson touched the young boy's arm. "Why don't you go ask Boone to play chess with you?"

"It is okay?" Samuel asked, his dark gaze on Raina. He spent most of his waking hours shadowing her around the house, hopping from one room to another, doing everything he could to help her with chores.

"Of course it's okay," Raina said with a gentle smile. "But remember, we need to leave in less than an hour."

"I will remember." Samuel grabbed crutches that were resting upright against the wall and left the kitchen, his narrow shoulders already looking a little stronger and broader than they'd been when he'd arrived. It was amazing what a little good food and a lot of affection could do for a child.

"Okay. The kid's gone," Chance said impatiently. "So, spill. What's the deal on Kent's wife?"

"According to a neighbor, she took a handful of sleeping pills, locked herself in the car while Kent was at work and killed herself."

"Did she leave a note?" Chance pressed for more information, but Jackson didn't have much. He'd spoken to a neighbor and to Cheryl's sister. According to them, police hadn't found anything suspicious about the death and the coroner had ruled it a suicide. Cheryl's sister had questioned that, hinting that there might have been more to the story than the obvious. When Jackson had pressed her for clarification, she'd clammed up and told him she had to go.

He wasn't sure what that meant, and since she hadn't taken any more of his calls, he didn't think he'd be getting an answer from her anytime soon. Hopefully, Wallace would have more luck. "No note. Apparently, not even a hint that she was suicidal. According to her sister, she was alive and happy one day and gone the next."

"That doesn't make sense," Raina said, grabbing the stack of plates Samuel had left and sliding them into the cupboard. "If she was happy, then why is she dead?"

"Her sister doesn't know. The neighbor speculated that she'd been depressed about not having kids. She'd been crying out on the front porch one day, and when the neighbor asked why, she'd said that she'd just found out she'd never have children."

"Sad," Chance interjected. "But not the end of the world."

"Maybe to her it was." Raina leaned a hip against the counter, her faded jeans clinging to long lean legs, her fingers tapping an impatient rhythm on her thigh. "I've known plenty of women who have gotten depressed about not being able to have biological children."

"How many of them took their own lives?" Chance intoned, his arms crossed over his chest, his expression neutral. Knowing him, he was calculating the odds, trying to figure out the statistics. As soon as they finished the conversation, he'd probably head to the computer and do the research, print out a bunch of information and then share it with the team later that night.

Jackson admired his brother's scientific approach to things, but he tended to work more on gut instinct and intuition. Right then, his intuition was telling him that a happily married woman with a good life and no sign of clinical depression didn't suddenly become suicidal because she couldn't get pregnant. "Wallace is looking into it. I was supposed to meet with him this afternoon, but I'll have to reschedule the meeting, though."

"Why would you do that?" Chance asked, glancing at his watch and frowning.

"Samuel has an appointment with the doctor."

"And?" His brother speared him with one of his famous you're-not-making-any-sense looks. Jackson ignored it.

"And Raina and Samuel need an escort."

"Boone and Stella can do it, and you and I can go to the meeting with Wallace. We need whatever information he has. The sooner we get it, the better."

"He's right," Raina interjected. "There's no need for you to reschedule, Jackson. Samuel and I will be fine."

Jackson ignored her comment, because he didn't want to leave her safety to someone else. Not even someone else who was part of the HEART family. "Boone and Stella can go to the meeting with Wallace. You and I can go to the medical appointment. That makes just as much sense as anything."

"Sure it does," Chance agreed. "Except Officer Wallace is expecting *you*. *You're* the one who's been gathering information, Jackson.

*You're* the one who spoke to Cheryl Moreland's neighbor and sister. *You're* one of the last people to see Butch alive. You're also the one who nearly got run down by the Jeep, chased a guy through the woods—"

"All right," Jackson cut him off. "I get your point."

"Then stop letting your emotions rule and do what needs to be done," Chance said. "I've got a couple of calls to make, but I'll be ready to leave when you are. We'll go as teams of two and meet up here or at the doctor's office when we're done, depending on how long the meeting with the police takes."

Jackson scowled, but his brother was already on his way out of the room and missed his irritated glare.

"Jackson." Raina touched his hand, her fingers skimming over his knuckles, that simple touch shooting warmth straight into his heart. "Don't compromise your job for my sake."

"This has nothing to do with my job, Raina. I'm on vacation. I can do what I want." But, of course, he really couldn't. Even on vacation, he was part of the team, part of the family that had been knit tightly together by passion and mission and heart.

"You know you can't." She smiled gently. "Not unless you want to spend Thanksgiving listening to your brother complain about your poor choices."

"Chance isn't like that." He captured her hand, tugging her closer. She smelled like sunlight and flowers, and he thought that if he had to, he could live on that scent and on her smiles. "He'll respect whatever choice I make."

"But will you?" She rested her palm on his cheek, her skin smooth and warm, her expression soft. "You know if I were anyone else, you'd already have left for your meeting."

"And?"

"And that's what I want you to do."

"Too bad it's not what *I* want to do."

"But it's what you *should* do. Your job isn't just something you do, Jackson. It's who you are. I'd never want you to compromise that for me."

He wasn't surprised by her words, but he *was* touched by them. In the years that he'd dated Amanda, he'd spent too much time feeling torn between his job and their relationship. Her neediness had drained him, sapped his energy and made him question whether or not he could ever have a lasting relationship. Since they'd broken up, he'd come to terms with the strain a job like his put on a relationship. He'd told himself over and over again that he didn't have the time that was necessary to make forever work.

He'd been wrong.

"You're a special lady, you know that?" he murmured, his lips brushing the soft skin behind her ear.

She shivered, melting into him, her arms sliding around his waist, her head resting against his chest. "I'm not special. I'm tired and scared, and I want all this to be over, so I can move on with my life."

"When it *is* over, I hope that moving on means moving toward me," he responded, easing back so he could look into her face, read the truth in her eyes. "Because I'm moving toward you, Raina, and I don't know what direction I'm going to head if that's not what you want."

She hesitated, and he could see the sadness in her gaze, knew she was thinking of her husband and her son and all the things she thought she had to leave behind to move forward. "I am moving toward you, Jackson. But it might take me a little longer to get there. I have a lot of stuff to deal with."

"I know, and I'm willing to wait for as long as it takes."

She smiled, her lips trembling, her eyes filled with tears. He wanted to kiss them away, to make her forget the sadness of what had been and embrace the joy of what could be. He cupped her nape, brushed her lips with his. He only meant it to be comforting, easy, light, but they both leaned closer, and the kiss became more than a light touch, more than a gesture that said "It's going to be okay."

Her lips tasted of sunshine and flowers and tears, and he wanted more. He wanted everything, because with Raina, he knew that was exactly what he would get. Heart, soul, passion, none of it withheld, none of it hidden.

Her hands slid up his back, her palms hot through his shirt, and he didn't want to stop, didn't want to think, just wanted to take the gift that he'd been given, the chance at what he'd thought he would never have.

# EIGHTEEN

"Hey, Raina! What time is that... Oh!" Stella's voice was like ice water in the veins, and Raina jumped back, slamming into the counter and stumbling forward again.

"Slow down," Jackson said, catching her waist and holding her steady. "You're going to hurt yourself."

"Man! Wow!" Stella stood in the threshold of the stairway, her eyes bright with amusement. "Didn't mean to interrupt. I wanted to check on the time for that appointment Samuel has."

"He has to be there at noon," Raina said, her voice a little rough, her breathing a little labored and, she was sure, her cheeks blazing red. "We should probably go."

"That's what I thought," Stella said, not even trying to hide her smile. "Of course, if you two want to hang out for a while longer, I can take the kid myself."

"No. He'll need me there."

"Okay. So, how about you go get him moving while I discuss the plan with Jackson?"

"Right. Sure." Raina met Jackson's eyes. "I guess I'll see you later?"

"You know you'll see me later," he promised, dropping a quick kiss on her lips. "But, as much as I hate to admit it, Chance is right. I need to be at that meeting with Wallace."

"You're meeting with that good-looking police officer?" Stella asked with a grin. "Maybe I should come along. Since I missed my date the other night, I'm in the market for a new guy."

"Sorry, Stella, but I need you to stay with Raina," Jackson said. "I'm counting on you to keep her safe. To keep them both safe."

All Stella's amusement fell away. Laughter left her voice and her eyes. She looked more serious than Raina had ever seen her. "I'll protect her and the kid with my life. You know that, Jackson."

He nodded, turning his attention back to Raina. "Make sure you stick close to Stella and Boone. I don't want anything to happen to you."

"I'll be fine," she assured him, but she felt anxious, worried, because he was worried and because she didn't think the calmness they'd had for the past few days was going to last.

"I'm counting on it." He dropped a quick kiss to her lips, gave her a gentle nudge toward the living room. "Go get Samuel. You don't want to be late."

She didn't, but she didn't really want to leave, either.

She felt right when she was with Jackson, complete in a way she hadn't been since the accident. The hole that her family's death had left was filling up, slowly flooding with new emotions, new people, new *hope*.

That's what had been missing from her life— hope in the future, belief that life still had wonderful things to offer, trust that God would take the bad and make good out of it.

Now that she had it, she wouldn't give it up.

She would have told Jackson that, but Samuel needed to be prodded away from the game of chess he was playing, and by the time she'd convinced him to brush his teeth and wash his face, Jackson and Chance had left.

There'd be time later.

Unless there wasn't.

That was the thing about life. Aside from the ones already lived, there were no moments guaranteed.

She shivered at the thought, hurrying Samuel out into the cold gray day. Muted sunlight filtered through the clouds but did nothing to warm the chilly air.

She unlocked the car, Stella and Boone hovering close by, gun holsters strapped to their chests and visible beneath their open coats. They looked tough and ready for trouble. For some reason, that didn't make Raina feel any less anxious.

The drive to the medical building took less than twenty minutes, the fall foliage vivid in the early-afternoon gloom. She parked close to the door, nearly tripping over her own feet as Stella hurried her inside and to the bank of elevators.

"We need to slow down," Raina panted. "Samuel can't keep up."

"He can when he's got a ride," Stella responded, gesturing toward the door. Boone strode in, Samuel in his arms. He set the boy down, handed him his crutches.

"I'm not liking this," he said, scanning the nearly empty lobby. "Things feel off."

"I was thinking the same." Stella punched the elevator button, her expression hard and unreadable. "Could be we're both just on edge. We're not used to being inactive for so long."

"Could be," Boone responded, but Raina didn't think he believed it.

*She* didn't believe it. Her skin felt tight, her hair standing on end as they got in the elevator and made their way to the third floor.

The radiology department was straight ahead, a

few patients waiting for their turns. Raina walked to the check-in desk, smiling at the receptionist.

"Name?" the gray-haired woman asked with a smile.

"Samuel Niag."

The receptionist typed something into her computer and frowned. "I see him on the schedule, but there's a note here that says you need to see his regular physician for a recheck on infection before we run the X-ray series, and I've got no referral on file."

"We were in to see Dr. Moreland two days ago," Raina responded. "He cleared Samuel for the X-rays and was supposed to fax the referral over."

"We didn't receive the paperwork for the consult. I can call Dr. Moreland if you'd like. Maybe he can fax something over."

"Actually, I work in his office. I'll go see if I can grab what you need and bring it to you."

"Are you sure, dear? It really isn't a problem for me to do it."

"I'm sure." Mostly because she knew exactly how long it could take for a fax to be sent, and she didn't want to spend any more time at the medical center than necessary. She walked to the seat Boone had set Samuel in. "Hey, buddy. I need to run and get something from Dr. Moreland. Do you think you can stay here with Boone for a few minutes?"

"Yes," Samuel said, but he was obviously anxious, his gaze darting around the room, his leg swinging with excess nerves.

"It's going to be fine," she said, crouching in front of him and looking into his eyes. "X-rays don't hurt a bit. You'll have them done, and when you come out, I'll be here waiting. Then we'll go to the library and get some books to bring home."

"No one said anything about a library," Stella said.

"We're going to the library," Boone responded. "The kid wants books, and he deserves them. He's a real trouper." He handed Samuel his phone, showed him a game he could play. "You two go ahead. I'll make sure the kid stays safe."

Raina hurried into the corridor, Stella at her side. "I don't understand why Kent didn't send the file over. He knows how important these X-rays are," she muttered.

"Because he's a self-centered jerk?" Stella offered.

"He's not self-centered." They rounded a corner, headed toward the east side of the building and the entrance to the clinic.

"Honey, trust me. I know self-centered when

I see it. The guy is way more interested in what he can get from you than what he can give."

"He's always been very good to me, Stella," she said, feeling obligated to defend the man.

"Because he wants something from you. That's the way men are. They act like princes until they have what they want. Then they act like slugs."

Stella pushed open the clinic door, gesturing for Raina to step in ahead of her. "Now listen," she said, pulling Raina to her side. "We stick together, okay? If there's trouble, you do what I say. No questions asked. Got it?"

"Got it," Raina said absently. She was more interested in getting the file and getting back to Samuel than she was in Stella's warnings. They were on her home turf, standing in an office she'd spent a good portion of the past three years in. As far as she was concerned, the clinic was almost as safe as home.

"Hey, Raina!" the receptionist said as she approached the front desk. "What's up?"

"I brought Samuel over to radiology, but they haven't received the referral."

"Wish I could help you with that, but I'm clueless. Kent is on break, though. If you want to go back to his office, I'm sure he can get it for you."

"Thanks."

"I'll let him know you're heading back." The

receptionist lifted the phone and punched a button. Seconds later, she hung up. "He said he'll be right up."

"Why not just let you go back there?" Stella muttered under her breath. "See what I mean? Self-centered. He wants to make a big show of being in control."

"I don't care what he's doing, as long as I get the referral."

"I care, and I might just tell him that when he finally shows his face. As a matter of fact—"

"Raina!" Kent appeared behind the receptionist, his white lab coat immaculate, an obviously fake smile on his face. "Sorry for forgetting to fax the referral. It's been hectic around here with you gone."

Raina didn't know how that could be, since people were filling her shifts, but she kept the thought to herself. "It's no problem, Kent, but Samuel's appointment is today, and I really need it."

"Come on back to my office. I'll get it for you." He took her arm, his grip just a little tighter than she would have liked. Her skin crawled, and she would have pulled back and refused to go if Stella hadn't been following along behind.

"So," Kent said as they stepped into his office, "how have things been going?"

"I guess as well as can be expected. Samuel seems to be adjusting well and—"

"I didn't mean with Samuel. I meant with you." He gestured to the chairs that sat in front of his desk. "Go ahead and have a seat. I need to get the referral form."

"I think I'll stand," Stella responded coldly.

"Suit yourself," Kent said, shoving his hands deep into the pocket of his lab coat and shrugging. "I'll ask Mandy to help me find the forms. Unless you want to come and look for them, Raina. You probably know where they—"

"She's going to stay here with me," Stella cut him off, her eyes as hard and cold as ice.

"No problem." Kent shrugged and headed for the door.

Somehow, his feet tangled up, and he stumbled forward, knocking into Stella. She shoved him away, hissing softly and grabbing her upper thigh.

"What do you have in that pocket, Doc? A—" She went pale, every bit of color draining from her face.

Raina lunged toward her.

"Don't bother." Kent grabbed her arm, pulling her away as Stella crumbled to the floor.

"What happened? What did you do?"

"Shut up!" he snarled, pulling out a gun and aiming it straight at her heart. "Because if you don't, I will kill everyone in this building, including that little brat you seem to love so much."

"Kent—"

"I said shut up!" He waved the gun wildly, and she froze. "That's better. Now we're going to walk out of here together. If anyone asks where we're going, you say we're heading to radiology."

"Stella—"

"Don't worry about her. She'll be conscious in a couple hours with nothing more than a headache to deal with."

"But—"

"Do you want people to die, Raina? Is that what you want? Because it's not that hard to take someone's life. It's really not."

She went ice-cold at his words, and did what he said, walking out of the room and out of the building, her heart beating frantically.

She had to escape. Had to—

Something slammed into the back of her head, and she fell, every thought falling into darkness with her.

# NINETEEN

"Open your eyes," a man said, the words seeping into her consciousness.

"Jackson?" she whispered, the word thick on her tongue, her head pounding.

"Hurry up. I don't have all day." A vicious slap stung her cheek, and she shot upright, her heart racing as memories flooded back.

Kent stood a few feet away, still in his lab coat, a cup of water in his hand.

"Where are we?" she asked, her throat clogged with fear.

"Don't you know?" He grinned, and everything evil she'd ever dreamed of was in that one little smile.

"No."

"Don't be obtuse, Raina. Look around."

She did. Saw old beige carpet and a baby grand piano that had been covered with a sheet. A fireplace. A small alcove that she knew had once contained a display table and tiny little angel figures.

Her in-laws' old house.

The knowledge shot through her. "What do you want, Kent?"

"What I wanted was you, but you didn't want me."

"I wasn't ready. I was still grieving Matt," she responded, easing toward the foyer. She made it to the threshold, the door just a few feet away. The dining room she'd eaten dozens of meals in just across the hall, the window allowing watery light to seep in. A shadow moved past. She blinked and it was gone.

Imagination or reality? She didn't know. Wasn't sure it mattered. Kent had a gun, and she was trapped inside with him. She reached for the door handle.

"There's no sense trying that door, Raina. I came in the back way. Broke the lock yesterday and set this all up." He gestured to dozens of rose petals that lay on the floor nearby. "I'm sure when they find you here, they'll figure it was your handiwork. Of course, they might not find you for a while. The house hasn't had many showings in the past few months."

"You're crazy," she spat, her voice trembling with fear.

"I'm not crazy. I'm angry. I don't like to be

ignored, Raina," he said, his voice silky and soft and so terrifying Raina wanted to lie back down on the floor, close her eyes, pretend the nightmare away.

*God, please, help me.*

The prayer was as desperate as her prayers in Africa had been, the danger she was in just as real. Only there was no little boy with a water bottle in his hands, no helicopter flying in to rescue her. No Jackson, lifting her into his arms.

She blinked back tears, forced back fear.

A soft sound broke through the silence. Fingers on glass? She turned her head, looking at the window again. Nothing. No face in the window there. No sign that help had arrived.

"Did you hear me?" he snapped. "I don't like to be ignored."

"I've never ignored you," she said, knowing that reasoning with him was futile, but hoping, praying, trusting that help was on the way.

"Drink this." He thrust the glass into her hands.

"What is it?"

"Death," he said, leaning toward her and inhaling deeply. "I'll miss you, Raina. I had high hopes that you were the one. After our time in Africa—"

"What time? We were trapped in separate cages. We never even spoke." She had to keep him talking, had to give herself more time. Give Jackson more time. He'd find her. She had to believe that. Had to believe that God hadn't brought her this far to let her die.

"We were the only survivors, because we were meant to be," he hissed. "I suspected you were mine after your husband died, and I knew it was true after Africa. God wanted us together, but you ruined it."

"I didn't know," she said, easing to the left, stepping farther into the foyer. She could see the kitchen from there, the back door beckoning.

"Because you ignored God!" he shouted so loudly the chandelier in the foyer rattled. "Worse, you ignored me! No one ignores me. Ever! Now drink or die with a bullet in your head." He pulled the gun from his pocket. "You choose."

"Okay." She lifted the glass, praying, trusting, hoping, even though she wasn't sure there was any hope left.

He smiled, the gun lowering a fraction of an inch.

That was her chance and she took it, throwing the glass at his head, and taking off down the hall, running from him, running toward Samuel, toward Jackson—toward life.

Glass shattered, and the world exploded into chaos. Voices. Shouts. But she kept running.

Something slammed into her shoulder. She stumbled into the kitchen and out into watery sunlight. Ran across the yard, voices shouting behind her, feet pounding behind her. She kept going, because she'd finally found the strength to live again, and there was no way she was going to give that up.

"Raina." Someone grabbed her arm, and she swung around, fists flying, head pounding, fear giving her the adrenaline she needed to fight. To win.

"Stop! You've been shot. You're going to bleed to death if you don't hold still!" It was Jackson's voice, frantic and filled with fear.

She stilled, looked into his eyes, her head swimming, her body numb. "It's okay," she said, touching his face, her hand slipping away because she didn't have the strength to hold it there.

"No," he ground out. "It's not okay. Get me something to stop this bleeding!" he shouted, and Boone appeared at his side, his red hair mussed, his eyes blazing.

"If Moreland weren't already dead," he said softly as he leaned toward Raina and pressed a thick wad of cloth to her shoulder. "I would kill him."

She thought that he meant it, but her head was so fuzzy, her thinking so scattered, she couldn't be sure. "Where's Samuel?"

"With Stella." Jackson brushed hair from Raina's cheek with one hand, pressed down on her shoulder with the other. His hands shook, his heart racing so fast he thought it might fly out of his chest. The bullet had hit an artery, and if he didn't stop the bleeding, she'd die. Not in a shoddy little village in Africa. Right there in her hometown.

He gritted his teeth, angry with himself for letting her go to the clinic, angry with Wallace for not making his first shot a killing shot.

He glanced at Wallace. He stood a few feet away, his face almost as ashen as Raina's.

"I should have taken him out," Wallace mumbled.

*That was the plan,* Jackson wanted to say. They'd gone over it all, briefed everyone. Just like with every mission. Every team member had a job, a position, a common goal.

Only Wallace wasn't a team member, and he hadn't shot to kill. He'd given Moreland the time he'd needed to fire his weapon. It was Chance who'd taken Moreland down. He'd broken protocol by doing it, leaving his position and firing before the doctor could take another shot.

"It's not your fault," Raina said, her eyes drifting closed. "You didn't know Kent had a gun."

"Don't!" Jackson shouted, and she opened her eyes again, reached for his hand and squeezed it.

"I'm going to be okay."

"You're bleeding like a stuck pig!"

"Again?" She smiled, then grimaced. "This hurts more than my head ever did."

"Yeah. I bet. And it's about to hurt worse," Chance muttered, kneeling beside Jackson, covering his hand and adding pressure to the wound.

Raina winced, but she didn't complain. She knew how quickly a person could bleed out, and she knew she could easily be one of them. Jackson could see it in her eyes. Not fear. Acceptance and a hint of sadness.

"You'll take care of Samuel for me, won't you?" she asked, her lips colorless, her skin almost gray.

"I'm not going to have to," he ground out, his heart nearly pounding from his chest. She closed her eyes again, and he glanced over his shoulder. "Where's the ambulance?"

"Pulling up. I'll lead them back," Boone shouted, running to the front of the house.

The rest happened in minutes, the crew moving in, shoving him aside as they worked to stop the bleeding and to stabilize Raina. He could see the panic in the EMTs faces, knew they thought they were going to lose her. He moved toward them, wanting to tear them away, move in close, tell her that she had better not even think about leaving him.

"Stay out of the way, bro." Chance grabbed his shoulder. "Let them do their job."

"What if doing their job isn't enough?" He yanked away, took a step toward Raina.

"That's up to God to decide." Boone stepped in front of him. "But you getting in the way isn't going to help and it might hurt. Seeing as how the mission was to get her out alive, I'm not going to let you do that."

If anyone else had been saying it, Jackson would have barreled past, but it was Boone, and he knew exactly what it was like to watch someone he loved slip away. "I can't lose her."

"You're assuming you're going to, and that's no way to think. Not when she's lying right there, still breathing and fighting. So, how about you stop thinking about you, and start thinking about what she really needs? I can guarantee it isn't you pouncing on a bunch of people who are trying to help her."

The words cooled the fire that was burning in Jackson's stomach, stilled the panic that had filled his brain.

"You're right," he acknowledged, and Boone stepped aside, motioned for him to move past.

"Looks like they're ready to transport her. You go on with her. I'll go back to the clinic and get Stella and the kid."

Jackson barely heard. He was already moving toward the gurney that was being wheeled across the grass and onto the ambulance. An IV line had been placed, fluid already pumping into Raina's arm. She looked small and vulnerable and incredibly pale, but she opened her eyes when he touched her hand, smiled through the oxygen mask that had been placed over her mouth. "It's going to be okay," he said, his voice rough as sandpaper. "*You're* going to be okay."

She turned her hand and captured his, her grip stronger than he'd expected, her eyes staring straight into his.

He knew what she needed, what she probably wanted more than anything.

"I'll take care of Samuel," he said.

And she squeezed his hand, smiled again.

"I knew you would," she said, her voice weak and a little hollow.

He leaned close, speaking in her ear so she could hear over the sound of screaming sirens. "But just until you get out of the hospital and only if you promise to teach me how to make that peach pie you said we'd have for Thanksgiving. I want to impress Great-grandma when she's here."

"I promise," she said, and he knew that she meant it, prayed that she could keep it.

She closed her eyes, but her grip on his hand didn't loosen as the ambulance sped toward the hospital. He held on tight, as if doing so could keep her from drifting away, as if any amount of effort on his part could keep her with him.

When the ambulance finally pulled up to the emergency room, an EMT almost had to pry Jackson's hand from Raina's.

She opened her eyes, looked confused and scared and a little panicked. And Jackson leaned close, whispered into her ear, saying what he should have said before, saying what needed to be said just in case there wasn't another chance to say it. "I love you, Raina."

He wasn't sure, but he thought he heard her say, "I love you, too," as they wheeled her away.

# TWENTY

Making pie crust one-handed wasn't easy.

Somehow, having extra help had only made it more difficult.

They'd managed, though, and Raina couldn't stop smiling as she looked at the broken crusts and misshapen pies she and Samuel had set out on the buffet table. Soon her less-than-beautiful pies would be joined by the food Jackson's family was bringing. According to Stella, they'd arrived in D.C. the day before, and had taken over Jackson's apartment. He'd driven back home after spending the day helping Raina make pies and had been forced to spend the night with Chance at the HEART office.

Raina smoothed a hand down her simple black dress. Jackson had told her to dress casually, but she wanted to impress his family. She hoped the black dress and lone strand of pearls would do it.

"You are beautiful," Samuel said. "This Thanksgiving is beautiful." He whirled around on his crutches, doing a fancy maneuver that made Raina laugh.

"It is, isn't it?"

"Jackson will be here soon?"

"I think so." She glanced at the clock. He'd said he'd be there an hour before his family, but he hadn't called to say he was leaving D.C.

"I think we will get married," Samuel announced, hopping over to the table and looking longingly at the pie.

"You and the pie?"

"No!" Samuel laughed, the sound the most beautiful song Raina had ever heard. "You and Jackson and me."

"Well…actually…"

The doorbell rang.

Saved by the bell!

"We'll talk about it later." She ran to the door, ignoring the slight throbbing in her shoulder. It opened before she reached it, cold air sweeping in as Jackson stepped through the doorway.

He looked good.

So good she threw herself into his arms.

He lifted her carefully, kissed her squarely on the mouth, then set her down again. "I have bad news."

"What? Is your family not coming?" She wasn't sure if she'd be relieved or disappointed if that were the case.

"Worse. I overslept my alarm this morning and didn't wake up until Mom called and asked directions to your place. They were right behind me all the way here."

"What? I don't even have the silverware out." She darted toward the kitchen, but he snagged the back of her dress and pulled her to a stop.

"Great-grandma brought her silverware and her china."

"But—"

"And I suggested Chance take them on a scenic tour of the town. That should buy us about ten minutes. I don't think Mom and the grandmas will let Chance drive around for any longer than that."

"I'd better hurry, then. I still need to—"

He pressed a finger to her lips, sealing the words. "You need to relax. My family doesn't need fancy. They don't need perfect. They just need love, and I think you've got plenty of that to go around."

"You're right," she said. "But I still wish I had some extra time. I wanted everything to be ready when they got here." She glanced around the great room. The buffet table was out and the folding chairs that she'd borrowed from the church placed strategically around the room.

It looked nice, but she'd wanted to have a

fire going and some music playing. "Maybe I should—"

"Stand right here with me and thank God that we have this day? It could have been a lot different."

"I know," she said, his words stealing away her nerves and insecurities. She'd almost died more than once in the past year, but she was here in her house with two people who she loved and who loved her. That couldn't take away the heartache of her loss, but it *could* fill the emptiness if she let it.

She wanted to let it.

"I was thinking," Jackson whispered in her ear. "That if we don't cut into that pie and eat a piece now, we might not get any. My family can put down some food. Not to mention Boone. He'll put away one of those pies all by himself."

"Is that why you really came early?" she asked with a laugh. "To steal a piece of pie before it's gone."

"I came early," he said, his expression suddenly serious, his eyes the deepest, darkest blue of the midnight sky, "because I love my family, but once they get here, they're going to steal you away from me."

"We'll have other days."

"We will, but they won't be like today." He

glanced at Samuel, who was standing at the buffet table, his gaze locked on the pies. "A day when a boy gets to experience his first Thanksgiving and a man gets to watch the woman he loves meet his family. A day when the past is only the past and the future is something to hope and dream about." He touched her cheek, his fingers gentle and warm. "A day when everything I've ever hoped for is standing right in front of me."

"Jackson—"

"I love you, Raina, and I'm not afraid to let my family, my friends and the world know, but I wanted to come early to make sure *you* knew, because that's all that really matters to me."

Her heart swelled at his words, filling up with a million dreams she'd thought had died.

They were there in his eyes just waiting for her to believe in them again.

"I love you, too," she whispered, and he leaned in and kissed her with passion and longing and love.

When he broke away, she was breathless, joyful, ready for whatever the future would bring.

"See?" Samuel said from his place at the buffet table. "I told you we were going to get married."

"Samuel, he hasn't asked me to marry him."

"Yet," Jackson said with a smile, hooking his arm around her waist and tugging her across the room. "But only because my great-gran would withhold her sweet potato casserole if I didn't wait until she was here."

Her pulse jumped at his words, at the look in his eyes.

"Speaking of which," he continued, "I do believe I hear my father's old Cadillac coughing its way up the road. I think our time is up. Come on, Samuel. Let's open the door together."

He kept his arm around Raina's waist, put a hand on Samuel's shoulder, and they stood in the open doorway, autumn sun streaming through colorful foliage as a caravan of cars pulled into the driveway.

Larry crossed the road with a bag in his hand, joining the throng of people who were moving toward Raina. Her eyes burned with the joy of it, her empty house filling with people, her empty heart filling with love, all the trouble and sorrow of the past finally leading her to the place God wanted her to be.

A good place.

A *great* place.

A better place than she could ever have imagined.

She squeezed Jackson's hand, looking into his eyes and smiling as a dozen people ran up the porch stairs, their laughter and joy spilling into the house and straight into Raina's overflowing heart.

\* \* \* \* \*

Dear Reader,

Many years ago, my brother almost disappeared from our lives. We were at a crowded tourist area when he was snatched from his stroller. Through God's grace, my father spotted my brother on the shoulders of the man who had taken him. Today, my brother is an Army Chaplain, helping those who are hurting and wounded. I can't imagine what life would be like if he had not been recovered and brought back to us. Through the experience of almost losing him, I got a very small glimpse of what families go through when their loved ones are missing.

*Protective Instincts* is the first book in my Mission: Rescue series. Each story centers around HEART—a hostage rescue team devoted to rescuing victims and reuniting families. I hope that you enjoy reading Raina and Jackson's story. If you have time, drop me a line at shirlee@shirleemccoy.com.

Blessings,

Shirlee McCoy

## Questions for Discussion

1. Raina Lowery's faith was shaken after her husband and son were killed in a car accident. What does she do to try to strengthen it?

2. Why did Raina quit her job as an E.R. nurse?

3. Do you think that the mission trip was part of God's plan for Raina's life? Why or why not?

4. Why was HEART formed?

5. How would you describe Jackson's relationship with his brother? With his family?

6. Jackson has a very strong faith. Did losing his sister affect that?

7. Have you ever lost someone close to you? What was your response? Did the experience draw you closer to God or make you question Him?

8. What is it about Jackson that Raina finds attractive? How does she feel about that attraction?

9. Jackson is convinced that he will never find a woman who will understand his passion for his job or the time that he must devote to it. What is it about Raina that makes him think she will understand?

10. What was Raina's motivation for seeking a medical visa for Samuel? How does she feel about cleaning out her son's room for him?

11. Raina doesn't believe that she can have a second chance at love. How about you? Do you believe it is possible to have more than one great love in a lifetime?

# LARGER-PRINT BOOKS!

## GET 2 FREE LARGER-PRINT NOVELS
## PLUS 2 FREE MYSTERY GIFTS

*Love Inspired*®

### Larger-print novels are now available...

**YES!** Please send me 2 FREE LARGER-PRINT Love Inspired® novels and my 2 FREE mystery gifts (gifts are worth about $10). After receiving them, if I don't wish to receive any more books, I can return the shipping statement marked "cancel." If I don't cancel, I will receive 6 brand-new novels every month and be billed just $5.24 per book in the U.S. or $5.74 per book in Canada. That's a savings of at least 23% off the cover price. It's quite a bargain! Shipping and handling is just 50¢ per book in the U.S. and 75¢ per book in Canada.* I understand that accepting the 2 free books and gifts places me under no obligation to buy anything. I can always return a shipment and cancel at any time. Even if I never buy another book, the two free books and gifts are mine to keep forever.

122/322 IDN F49Y

| | |
|---|---|
| Name | (PLEASE PRINT) |

| | |
|---|---|
| Address | Apt. # |

| | | |
|---|---|---|
| City | State/Prov. | Zip/Postal Code |

Signature (if under 18, a parent or guardian must sign)

### Mail to the **Harlequin® Reader Service:**
**IN U.S.A.:** P.O. Box 1867, Buffalo, NY 14240-1867
**IN CANADA:** P.O. Box 609, Fort Erie, Ontario L2A 5X3

**Are you a current subscriber to Love Inspired books
and want to receive the larger-print edition?
Call 1-800-873-8635 or visit www.ReaderService.com.**

\* Terms and prices subject to change without notice. Prices do not include applicable taxes. Sales tax applicable in N.Y. Canadian residents will be charged applicable taxes. Offer not valid in Quebec. This offer is limited to one order per household. Not valid for current subscribers to Love Inspired Larger-Print books. All orders subject to credit approval. Credit or debit balances in a customer's account(s) may be offset by any other outstanding balance owed by or to the customer. Please allow 4 to 6 weeks for delivery. Offer available while quantities last.

**Your Privacy**—The Harlequin® Reader Service is committed to protecting your privacy. Our Privacy Policy is available online at www.ReaderService.com or upon request from the Harlequin Reader Service.

We make a portion of our mailing list available to reputable third parties that offer products we believe may interest you. If you prefer that we not exchange your name with third parties, or if you wish to clarify or modify your communication preferences, please visit us at www.ReaderService.com/consumerschoice or write to us at Harlequin Reader Service Preference Service, P.O. Box 9062, Buffalo, NY 14269. Include your complete name and address.

LILPDIR13R

# *Reader Service*.com

## Manage your account online!

- Review your order history
- Manage your payments
- Update your address

---

*We've designed
the Harlequin® Reader Service
website just for you.*

---

## Enjoy all the features!

- Reader excerpts from any series
- Respond to mailings and
  special monthly offers
- Discover new series available to you
- Browse the Bonus Bucks catalog
- Share your feedback

*Visit us at:*
## ReaderService.com